‘Better to be
in Italy with
passion for y

‘You have no id
cheeks flushed wi

‘You assured me he had no amorous intentions. What a waste.’

‘If I were on my feet you wouldn’t say things like that,’ she said primly.

‘Of course I would,’ Alain assured her, his dark eyes gleaming with malicious amusement. ‘I am French, *mademoiselle*. We are not a cold-blooded race.’

Next month sees a great new look for our Romances—and we can guarantee you'll enjoy our stories just as much. Passionate, sensual, warm and tender—at heart, Mills & Boon Romances are as satisfying as ever.

THE EDITOR

Dear Reader

Bienvenue en France! This is a country that has everything lovers might require. From the glamour and beauty of the Riviera, to the rolling countryside and unspoilt medieval towns of the wine-growing Périgord, and the grandeur and romance of Paris, its capital city. . .with its delicious food and fine wines. . .France is a feast of the senses, with that certain *je ne sais quoi* that gives romance a real sparkle!

The Editor

The author says:

To me France is superb food, rich wines, boulevard cafés and colourful village markets. From its beautiful châteaux to the vast forests and mountains, this country of style and sophistication is a place of plenty for any visitor. The rich history of its towns, its treasures and of its culture forms a wonderful contrast to the way of life of modern France. To know France is to enjoy the delights of contact with a hospitable and generous people and to share with them the pleasures of a country so gifted in natural beauty.

Patricia Wilson

★ TURN TO THE BACK PAGES OF THIS BOOK FOR *WELCOME TO EUROPE*. . .OUR FASCINATING FACT-FILE ★

A HEALING FIRE

BY

PATRICIA WILSON

MILLS & BOON LIMITED
ETON HOUSE 18–24 PARADISE ROAD
RICHMOND SURREY TW9 1SR

First published in Great Britain 1993
by Mills & Boon Limited

This edition 1993

ISBN 0 263 78219 0

Set in 10 on 11 pt Linotron Plantin
01-9309-60193

Typeset in Great Britain by Centracet, Cambridge
Made and printed in Great Britain

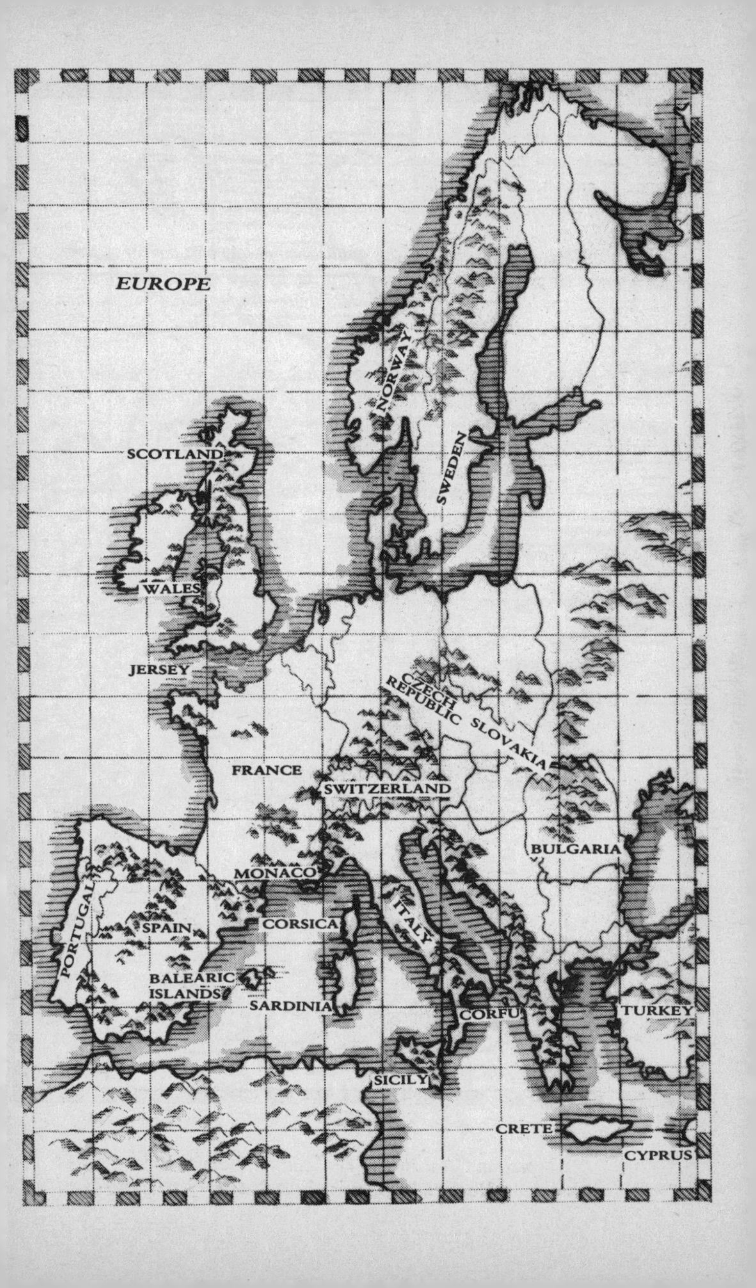
EUROPE
NORWAY
SWEDEN
SCOTLAND
WALES
JERSEY
CZECH REPUBLIC
SLOVAKIA
FRANCE
SWITZERLAND
BULGARIA
MONACO
PORTUGAL
SPAIN
CORSICA
ITALY
BALEARIC ISLANDS
SARDINIA
CORFU
TURKEY
SICILY
CRETE
CYPRUS

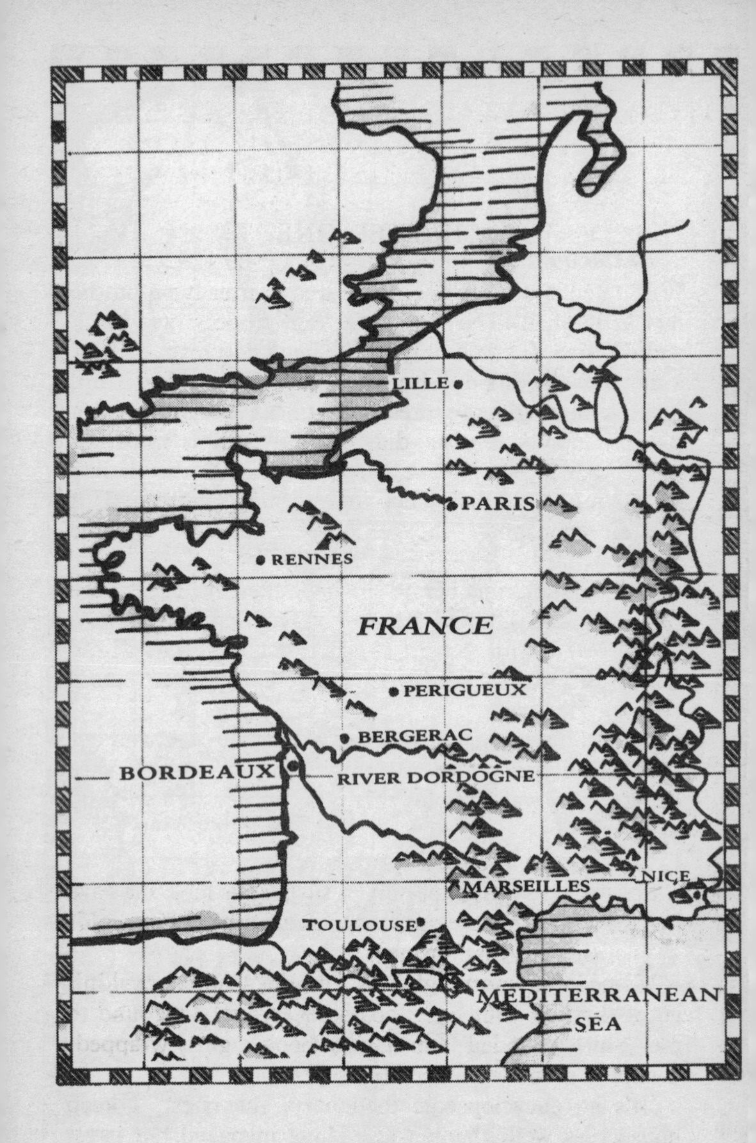
LILLE
PARIS
RENNES
FRANCE
PERIGUEUX
BERGERAC
BORDEAUX
RIVER DORDOGNE
NICE
MARSEILLES
TOULOUSE
MEDITERRANEAN
SEA

CHAPTER ONE

WHEN Jenna came home, there was a letter lying on the mat in the hall. The writing on the envelope was black and decisive. It could only be the hand of a man, and for a moment she stood quite still, hesitating to pick it up, filled with a gloomy presentiment. It bore a French stamp and suddenly she didn't want to know what was inside that letter. It gave her great qualms that it had been lying in the hall since the morning's post, as if it had an atmosphere capable of permeating the whole house.

The doorbell rang before she had taken even one more step and she jumped nervously, coming out of her anxious state with a start. It was ridiculous, but, all the same, she pushed the letter into her pocket before opening the door.

It was Shirley, her neighbour, with more post, and her appearance brought a smile of relief to Jenna's face because this was normal, this was the new life with no past.

'You're pale. Not peaky, are you?'

Shirley gave Jenna the sort of suspicious look she gave her children when they sniffed with an approaching cold.

'Just tired. Is that for me?'

'Came in the morning's post, but the postman couldn't get it through your letter-box so he brought it round to me.' Shirley handed Jenna a huge book, tightly wrapped. 'I hope it's a book on good housekeeping.'

'It's an encyclopaedic dictionary, the latest. I keep house very well, thank you.' Jenna managed her usual smile, but the letter seemed to be controlling her, burning a hole in her pocket, and, for once, she wanted to get rid of Shirley fast.

'I'm waiting for you to announce the wedding. I've got two little bridesmaids next door.'

'They'll have a long wait,' Jenna laughed. 'I'm not even engaged yet. Never mind, they can be matrons of honour when I decide to tie the knot.'

'Left to you, I expect they'd be old enough,' Shirley mused. 'I can't see Glyn Rushton waiting that long though. What do you want to be all alone in this house for when there's a man ready to marry you? He's got it made, too—big house, big firm, pots of cash.'

'He's my friend,' Jenna pointed out firmly, standing her ground. If she backed away into the kitchen then she would never get rid of Shirley and tonight she had promised to cook dinner for Glyn. 'Are the girls home from school?' she enquired with a burst of inspiration.

'They are. I left them eating their tea. Oh! I forgot. It's Brownie night. I'll have to go!'

Jenna smiled to herself and shut the door. She knew it was Brownie night, otherwise she wouldn't have been able to get Shirley out until her long-suffering husband came home. At this moment she didn't really need a neighbour, not even a good one. The letter was waiting, lying in her pocket in a demanding way as if it had control of her.

She took it out, not looking at it as she walked into the kitchen, tearing the envelope as she went. Who could be writing from France? Her connection with France was tenuous to say the least—a fragile link broken long ago. Her mouth twisted wryly; at twenty-four she should have put all that aside, but it lingered on like a bitter legacy. Just the sight of the stamp had been enough to set her heart beating uneasily and she had to fight down the urge to put off reading the words someone had written to her.

It took her several seconds to absorb the letter although it did not in any way fill the one sheet of paper.

Mademoiselle Bryant,
It is my duty to inform you that your father is very dangerously ill. He is not expected to live very long. It could be a matter of weeks. Naturally he has expressed a desire to see you, but if his wishes are to be fulfilled you must leave for France at once. Please ring me at the above number and I will meet you in Paris to escort you to the hospital.

She dropped the letter on the kitchen table, staring at it bleakly, her eyes almost mesmerised by the one name—Lemarchand. How was it that after so long that name could strike out at her, bringing back the long lost desolation, the raw feeling of rejection?

There were no condolences, no flowery words, nothing but stark fact, not even the normal ending. He merely signed his name at the bottom of the sheet, firm, black and imperious. Alain Lemarchand.

Her mother's face came swimming into her mind, blotting out the sight of the message from so far away. It would never be her father's face that materialised; how could it be? She had been eight years old and that was sixteen years ago. Even if he looked the same, she could not remember him. She only remembered her mother and the grief that the name Lemarchand had brought.

Every instinct warned her to tear the letter up, to burn it, to destroy it and never think of it again. Her father would not remember her either because she was no longer eight years old and heartbroken. Why should he want to see her? He had not wanted to see her once in all the long years.

It took a great mental effort to move and go upstairs to change; even then, she had to keep her mind blank, and it was only as she cooked the evening meal, every action mechanical, that she thought clearly again.

How had this man found her? How did he know anything about her? Until she was sixteen they had been constantly moving and there had never been anyone left behind to pass on her address. Her father had never bothered to find out, so how had this Frenchman succeeded? It was too big a puzzle and she let it go although it gnawed away at the back of her mind.

Should she go to France? A last request? Could she face it in any case without showing the bitterness? They said that every action of life showed on the face, in the expression. Surely Russell Bryant must have some sign on him of his past life, then? Could a man who deserted his wife and child for another woman get off free without scars?

Her mother had borne scars. She had been coldly beautiful until the day she died, but nothing had brought her happiness. She had laughed, lived a perfectly normal life, shouldering the responsibility of being alone to bring up her daughter, but, with a child's uncanny insight, Jenna had known that her mother had never recovered.

When the initial grief of the desertion had passed she had known better than to mention her father's name. She was told the facts. Russell Bryant had gone to France to marry a French widow called Lemarchand. He cared nothing for his wife and daughter and they must wipe him from their minds.

Jenna had never known if that last advice had come from her mother or if it had been her father's order. If it was, he had certainly followed it scrupulously himself. Not once in the long years had he attempted to get in touch, to correspond with a daughter he had been all too ready to abandon.

And now he wanted to see her! It seemed almost a mockery, a travesty of what should have been. In her teenage years she had thought it out carefully. She had seen her friends with their own fathers and her more mature outlook had pinpointed the crime readily. People divorced, left each other—grown men and women who reached the decision to part. They clung to their children, though, sharing them equally, neither partner prepared to let go.

She had not been in that position. Her own father had left her readily, left her to an uncertain future, his love for some glamorous Frenchwoman overriding his love and duty to his own child. She had felt worthless, doubly deserted, and had finally wiped him from her mind, only a faint bitterness left, a hollow, incomplete feeling she would always carry.

Lemarchand! And who was Alain Lemarchand? A relative? The woman's brother? Did the woman herself feel too much guilt to write? Jenna left the meal to keep hot and went to freshen up, telling herself that she would consider it coldly and then decide, but in reality she was churned up inside, a desire to hide from this uppermost, but a deep-seated and almost morbid curiosity urging her to go to France and see the man who was nothing to her at all, not even a face to remember.

She had made her decision before Glyn came. She would not go. She would not get in touch with this Frenchman who had written so imperiously. She owed her father nothing, not even the duty to clear his guilty conscience at the end. She would not let one demanding letter fill her with guilt.

Glyn thought differently, his steady voice and cool logic urging her to see that she was refusing to face facts.

'You can't duck out of it, Jenna,' he pointed out. 'If you don't go, you'll have it at the back of your mind for the rest of your life, wondering what it would have been like to really know him. He won't even look the same. Apart from being old, he's ill, dying, but he's still your father.'

Jenna looked across at him as they sat with their coffee in the sitting-room that still bore the signs of her mother's impeccable taste. His face was serious. He never spoke without considering the implications—the result of his profession, she supposed, also the result of his steady character. He regarded her calmly through dark-rimmed spectacles and she felt a burst of unusual irritation.

'All the more reason not to go. He won't even know me. I've nothing to regret. I was never given a choice because he clearly didn't want me. Should I now go haring off to France to a man I don't know, a man who had no regrets for sixteen years?'

'How do you know?' He looked at her levelly. 'How can you tell what's been eating into him for all that time?'

'Easily. He never once tried to contact me. He never helped either. We had to constantly move when I was a child, from one house to another, one district to another, always trying to find cheaper houses.'

'Really?' Glyn looked round the firelit room. 'There are some valuable things in here. You don't look like a girl who has tasted any sort of deprivation; neither did your mother. I don't remember seeing Imogen looking anything but glamorous.'

'She covered things well and she was a good manager.' Jenna felt the rising of annoyance that came when any mention was made of her mother, and he let the subject drop at once, too well trained to antagonise.

'All the same. I think you should go, not for his sake but for your own, Jenna. Doesn't your school close for half-term in two days?'

'One day—tomorrow, in fact.'

'It doesn't leave you much excuse. We're not going to Italy for another week. You'll enjoy the holiday much more if you've been to France and faced your ghosts.'

Ghosts. Yes, she could see that they were ghosts. All these uneasy feelings that were at the back of her mind from time to time. The letter had brought them to the surface, where they could hurt more.

As he left, Glyn suddenly looked at her suspiciously.

'How did he know where to write?'

'I've been asking myself that question,' Jenna confessed, but all she got was another suspicious look.

'Have you been writing to him?'

'Are you out of your mind?' She was really angry with him at once. This apparently was a night for a lot of 'firsts'. 'How would I know where to write? My father hasn't been in touch since I was eight years old. It would never have occurred to me to try and get in touch with him. He deserted me!'

'Sorry.' Glyn looked abashed. 'It's a funny thing, though.'

It wasn't funny to Jenna. It was downright sinister and the fact that Glyn had picked up on her uneasy feelings left her more uneasy still. When he had gone she faced things all over again, glad to have the advice of someone so level-headed. Glyn was a lawyer, a partner in Rushton and Clarke, a firm who had been the family solicitors for several years, since her teenage years when she and her mother had come here and stopped roaming and moving at last. Glyn's father had retired two years ago and now Glyn had taken his place, working with Ned Clarke, who had been her mother's solicitor, a rather dour, calm-faced man who always slightly worried Jenna.

His age made him senior partner, and Gemma wished he were not. She found him pompous and annoying. He had dealt with everything when her mother died and he had dealt with it competently and in a kindly manner, but, left to herself, she would have gone to Glyn. Apparently, though, it was not etiquette, a reality laughingly pointed out to her by Glyn when they had started going out with each other on a regular basis.

This year Jenna was going on holiday with Glyn, a fact which brought a twinkle to the bright eye of her scheming neighbour Shirley, but they were not lovers, no matter what Shirley thought, and Jenna had pondered long and hard before agreeing to the holiday. She was not ready to place her life in the hands of any man. Her mother had done that and two people had suffered for it.

All the same, Glyn's advice was hard to dismiss, and

as Jenna got ready for bed in the silent house she reached the conclusion she had been pushing aside since the shock of the letter had settled. She would go. She had dismissed the instinctive feeling before, but it was still there, and Glyn had merely heightened it.

She faced her own image in the mirror as she brushed her hair. How would her mother have taken it if she had been alive? Would some lingering affection for the man she had once married have driven her to France to see him for the last time? Jenna did not have her mother's memories, she could not conjure up his face, and she knew that this fact alone would haunt her if she stayed away.

How would her father recognise her, beyond the name? She was tall, slim, fair like her mother had been, ash-blonde, her hair falling straight and beautiful to her shoulders. She had the fine, fair skin that went with it, the blue eyes, but her own eyes were dark blue, ringed by unusually dark lashes for one so fair. She knew she was too serious. It seemed long ago that she had left her teenage years behind and faced college and a job with determination.

Glyn suited her. He was steady, dedicated to his job as she was. There would be no women in Glyn's life, no turbulent affairs. It would be safe, secure, well planned. They had already started to look at houses—not any close inspection, just murmured approval as they had been driving, Glyn's comments warming her. 'We could extend that.' 'We could build a nice garden there.' The future settled with no sort of upheaval, not even a real discussion. She would have her job, he would have his. Life would be comfortable.

How comfortable had her mother's life been? For the first time, tonight, she had looked at her home, really looked at it after Glyn's observations. No, she didn't really remember being at all deprived. The deprivation had been the loss of her father, the constant loss of friends and contacts. Material things they had in plenty, and though they had moved to cheaper housing she could not actually remember feeling that they had moved down the social ladder at all. The houses and the district had never looked any cheaper.

In any case, the die was cast, she had made up her mind. Tomorrow she would telephone this Frenchman. She would telephone in her lunch-break. She hoped he spoke English as well as he wrote it and she hoped too that his slightly censorious tone did not surface as he met her in Paris. There had been something of a reproof in that letter, even though no word of it had been written openly. It had left her a little awe-stricken and she made a move to look at it again as it lay on her dressing-table.

She never completed the move. It had disturbed her enough, and even if the unwritten reproof had been solely in her own imagination she was not about to look again and check it. She stared uneasily at the envelope, at the black, firm hand, at the French stamp, and then she put out the light and went to bed. Tomorrow she would hear his voice and she was not looking forward to it. She knew it would take courage to ring that number.

Grey House was a very exclusive girls' school, and as she drove into the extensive grounds the next morning Jenna felt the peace of the place close over her as usual. She was happy here. Her very good degree and her dedication had earned her a place here the year before and now she taught English to girls who were only too willing to be taught. It was civilised, calm and elegant, the sort of surroundings she thrived in.

'Oh, Miss Bryant!' The school secretary came over as Jenna entered the main doors. 'The head asked me to let her know when you arrived. I think she wants a favour.'

They smiled at each other with complete understanding. It meant that Mrs Constantine had been asked to attend a meeting and wanted to get out of it at all costs.

She had lived in the lovely old building for twenty years and never had any desire to leave it or the grounds. Someone was always dragged in to delegate for her if the outside world called. This time, and not for the first time, it was to be Jenna.

She was still smiling as she got back into the car and headed for town. Mrs Constantine would take the English classes this morning if Jenna would just 'nip off' to town and attend the opening of the new bookshop. Who could refuse? Jenna was still smiling as she pulled into the market square and locked her car. There was a small, interested queue already lined up and the new manager shrugged his shoulders and smiled across. He hadn't really expected to actually see Mrs Constantine; she was gaining a rather eccentric reputation. His looks said it all, and Jenna suppressed a smile and set off across the road to join him.

She never saw the car. Someone screamed and the small queue scattered, but Jenna was already by the shop as the skidding car hit the plate-glass window. It all happened so fast that Jenna had no time to move. She was too stunned to really see the way the car shattered the wide expanse of glass and then she instinctively covered her face as jagged pieces flew out into the street. There was a searing pain in her leg and she fell.

For a second she blacked out, not from pain but from the shock of it all, and when she opened her eyes she was looking into a sea of faces all staring down at her. One of them was Glyn. His office was just across the square and the sight of him took some of the fright away.

'It's all right, Jenna,' he said in his matter-of-fact way. 'They've rung for an ambulance.'

'The glass?' She looked up at him, feeling strangely composed.

'Yes. Don't worry. They'll be here in a minute.'

'Actually, I'm not worrying,' Jenna murmured. 'I can't seem to feel anything. I'm a bit dazed, I think.'

'Loss of blood,' somebody said knowledgeably, and Glyn turned to glare at them. Not that it troubled Jenna. She felt light-headed and then she fainted. When she came round she was already in the local hospital, matters taken out of her hands.

Now I won't be able to phone France. The thought swam into her mind out of nowhere and she felt vaguely guilty when she realised it was a great relief to have this excuse. That letter had unnerved her and now she could not face speaking to the man who had written it. When she was out of here she would write to him and explain. If it wasn't too late she would go to France. It put off the facing of her ghosts, but it gave her conscience some respite.

'Sure you can manage?'

Shirley lingered in the sitting-room two weeks later and looked uneasily at Jenna.

'What's to manage? You've given me my breakfast, left my lunch on the kitchen table, cleaned the house and helped me down the stairs. Apart from standing up and sitting down there's nothing at all to do.'

'Well, I mean—with you so weak and vague. . .'

'Shirley! Do you mind? I'm not vague! It's only because I'm just out of hospital.'

'Well, don't go up those stairs,' Shirley ordered, making for the door. 'You're still weak. You might faint. You were lucky to get off so lightly, losing all that blood, and I'll be keeping an eye on you. I expect Mr Rushton will come and make dinner for you both tonight.'

Jenna didn't expect so herself. Glyn had come yesterday, but Shirley had already cooked, and he had looked extremely relieved at that. Glyn was not in any way domesticated. He felt that his job was quite sufficient. She had never even expected him to help with the dishes when she had fed him here. Somehow she would cope with the evening meal herself, but she kept silent about it. Shirley thought little of a man who couldn't 'turn his hand to anything'.

'We'll manage,' she murmured as Shirley got to the door.

The bell rang before she could open it and Jenna stood just inside the sitting-room in her long housecoat, wondering who on earth it could be; the post had arrived over an hour ago and she didn't know enough people to be expecting visitors. Only Glyn and Shirley had visited her in hospital. The constant upheaval of her life had parted her from any close friends and her own quiet, withdrawn manner kept most people at arm's length.

As Shirley opened the door, Jenna stiffened, her tall, slender figure held rigidly still, the back of the settee a firm place to grip with suddenly shaking fingers because for some inexplicable reason she knew who it was before he even attempted to speak. The ruggedly handsome face looked impatient and his size was quite intimidating.

He didn't even look at Shirley either. His dark eyes flashed straight across the hall and pinned Jenna mercilessly.

'Mademoiselle Bryant?'

How had he known? Jenna had never heard her own name said with so much accusation and all she could do was nod her head, words sticking in her throat at the blast of displeasure in the dark voice.

'Can I help you?' Shirley put in firmly, apparently hearing the tone of the voice herself. 'Miss Bryant is——'

'It's all right, Shirley,' Jenna managed quietly, her eyes held by the dark gaze. 'I'll see you later. I expect you're Monsieur Lemarchand?' she added, schooling herself to remain calm.

'I am, *mademoiselle*.'

'Then you'd better come in.' For the life of her she couldn't move and as Shirley left, her face alight with enquiry, Jenna motioned the tall dark stranger to come into the sitting-room.

He closed the outer door firmly and turned to look at her again. It was upsetting that he should have arrived on her very first real day back. Coming out of hospital was traumatic enough without facing the accusing man, and Shirley was quite right about the weakness.

His glance raked her from head to foot before he even moved further and she could see that he thought her very decadent to be in her housecoat at this time in the morning. She had needed to make a real effort to get up today at all. Sometimes she felt very tired. Things had not gone too smoothly in hospital and it was taking a long time to recover.

That he had to pass fairly close to her made Jenna's heart beat alarmingly and all she could think was that she wished she had phoned and spared herself this. She had even been going to write today as soon as Shirley had gone. Clearly he had not been content to wait, and as she looked at the hard, handsome face she knew he was furiously angry, only good manners holding back the words that were obviously uppermost in his mind.

Inside the sitting-room he spun round on her, standing across the room as if any contact with her would be an unpleasant episode in his life. He looked wealthy, assured, and he was beautifully dressed with the casual elegance of the men of his nationality.

He must have been well over six feet tall because Jenna was not in any way small, but she felt it now. His hair was almost black, heavy and smoothly groomed, swept back from a face that was icily cold, only the long, humorous-looking mouth telling her that this hostility was solely for her benefit and not some natural mannerism.

'You did not telephone and you did not arrive. As more than two weeks have passed, I presume you received my letter, Mademoiselle Bryant?'

'Yes. I did.' Jenna stood perfectly still and felt unable to look away or make any sort of move. Words of self-defence just would not come. She felt curiously defenceless, almost on the edge of tears.

'Then I can assume that you made your decision and that condolences are not required. Your father didn't live as long as the doctors expected. He died last night. You had just enough time to arrive and yet you chose not to do so.' The near-black eyes moved over her with open distaste. 'I need to return at once to deal with the funeral and, unless you intend to accompany me, we must discuss his affairs now.'

Still she felt unable to speak. In some odd way he was not a stranger because his name was painfully familiar and she imagined she had been expecting this angry arrival since her accident—that must be the cause of this feeling that was swimming through her. His letter had not contained any regrets for her forthcoming ordeal and he did not look like a man who would have much patience with women in any case. He made her feel shockingly vulnerable when she should have been consumed with annoyance herself. He had no right to take this attitude.

He looked at her with exasperation when she just gazed at him with wide deep blue eyes. His dark eyes flared over her hair and the long lips compressed in irritation as if the sight of her was more than enough to infuriate him.

'If you would sit, *mademoiselle*, and have the courtesy to invite me to do likewise, we can begin our tiresome but necessary discussion.'

'I'm sorry.' Soft apricot colour flared in her cheeks at this rasp of disapproval. 'I'm afraid I was taken by surprise. Please sit down, *monsieur*.'

'After you, Mademoiselle Bryant,' he insisted harshly, waiting with ill-concealed impatience and obviously wanting to speak his mind and depart swiftly.

Jenna hadn't realised just how weak she felt until that moment and she kept a firm grip on the back of the settee. They had told her in hospital that the glass had cut into an artery and she had needed transfusions but although she had felt far from well this morning she was certainly feeling worse now. He was making her anxious and that was no help at all.

As she moved slowly however it became apparent that her tall, slender stance was one of self-defence, not defiance, and she had not taken more than two steps when he was across the room hovering over her.

'*Mon Dieu*! You are ill! This is why you are so pale?'

He sounded unspeakably shocked, his voice low and urgent, and she would have liked to pretend that she was seriously ill. She would have liked to pay him back for his earlier tone by pretending a permanent disability. As it was, he was looking down at her, and she could do nothing but speak the truth.

'I'm not ill, *monsieur*, just tired. I was involved in an accident. I came home last night. I've been in hospital.'

'*Depuis quand*?'

Jenna looked up at him with puzzlement in her deep blue eyes and he shrugged with annoyance at this slide into his own language.

'Since when, *mademoiselle*? When did you have this accident?'

'Just over two weeks ago. The morning after I received your letter, Monsieur Lemarchand.'

'I see.' To her surprise he took her arm, his hand under her elbow, forcing her to place her weight firmly on him as he helped her to her seat. 'What kind of accident, *mademoiselle*?'

'A car went out of control and hit a plate-glass window. I happened to be there. The glass cut my leg.'

'And this is the only injury you sustained?'

He sat in the chair opposite and regarded her steadily. He looked elegantly at home, quite above this sort of thing, and she couldn't help wondering who he actually was and what he did for a living. He was about thirty-five or -six and, whatever he did, he was successful at it. There was an air of command about him that was quite alarming. From the beautifully groomed hair to the dark intensity of his eyes he spelled wealth, power and hauteur. She even had to struggle to answer him and he looked as if he knew it.

'Yes. It's quite enough to be going on with.'

'Had this not happened, you would have come to France?'

He looked as if he was encouraging her to say yes and then he could forgive her in a lofty sort of manner, and it annoyed Jenna instantly, partly driving away her unexpected awe of him. She didn't feel quite so bad now she was sitting down, and every instinct warned her to be on guard.

'I hadn't quite decided, *Monsieur*,' she lied. 'It was the last day of school and I had intended to phone you later although I hadn't decided what to say.'

'School?' For some reason he picked up on that word and let her cool statement go by for the moment.

'I'm a teacher, Monsieur Lemarchand. I teach English at a girls' school.' He just went on staring at her until she began to feel uncomfortable and agitated. Those dark eyes had softened considerably, but they seemed to be boring into her and she had a ridiculous urge to duck her head.

Instead, she looked straight at him.

'I think you'd better tell me why you're here, *Monsieur*.'

'Certainly, *mademoiselle*.' He sat back and released her from the probing examination, meeting her gaze more normally. 'I am here because you have a legacy from your father. Before I leave I must know what you intend to do about it.'

'A *legacy*?' Her father had been an artist and not at all successful according to her mother.

'A legacy, *mademoiselle*. A house in France. It is the

house that your father lived in for fifteen years. He lived there with my mother immediately after they married. I also lived there from time to time many years ago. It was a happy house, a house in the sun, but at the moment it is standing forlorn and empty because he is dead. You, however, are his daughter and the law does not forget you.'

Jenna just stared at him blankly, feeling not quite capable of absorbing this. Alain Lemarchand! This man was her *stepbrother*? Russell Bryant had married his mother, lived happily, had a house in the sun. The law did not forget her. Only her father had done that and he had obviously welcomed Alain Lemarchand just as he had rejected her. How old had her stepbrother been then? Twenty? Twenty-one? Old enough to take care of himself, while she had been eight years old.

The apricot flush stained her cheeks again but this time it was anger—anger and bitterness. She wanted nothing at all from her father and she was about to tell Alain Lemarchand so in no uncertain terms. If he liked the house so much he could go and live in it himself and relive his happy memories.

Her awe of him disappeared. At this moment she felt he had had a hand in cheating her out of some of her life, and the feeling made her coldly angry.

'I'm sorry you came so far for such a reason, Monsieur Lemarchand. Obviously lawyers will deal with the whole thing. A letter from them would have done perfectly well. I'm quite used to hearing from lawyers. My father seemed to be happy to conduct his affairs through them for long enough. I have a solicitor in England who will reply to them and give them instructions.'

For a second he looked across at her. There was this same probing again at her hardened tone, this summing up, and Jenna kept her face perfectly still, as icily cold as she could manage, although inside she was filled again with the same old grief, the same feeling of being worthless. It was a weakness that her father had left her with long ago and she had never conquered it. She didn't want another legacy.

'I came because I considered it to be my duty,' he informed her quietly. At the sight of her cold face any warmth that had grown had left his eyes. 'I understood that you were very young and——'

'Twenty-four is not very young, *Monsieur*!'

'To me it seems so,' he murmured sardonically, his gaze noting the new flush that stained her cheeks. 'However, young or not, I felt it my duty to see you and explain.'

'I can't see much to explain,' Jenna pointed out sharply. 'I've been left a house in France, end of subject, except that it is my intention——'

About to tell him hotly that she would not accept any legacy, Jenna was interrupted sharply, the words dying on her lips as he stood and began to pace about restlessly, hands in his pockets.

'Not quite, *mademoiselle*,' he pronounced firmly, spinning to face her. 'French laws of inheritance are unlike the law you are used to. You have a legacy and it is in property. You do not however now own a house in France. You own part of a house. Two other people share the house.'

'So my father didn't leave a will?' Even at the end he had not thought of her, and there was a quiet desolation on Jenna's face. He saw it. His changed expression showed her that clearly, and she knew too he put it down to greed.

'He did not. It would have made little difference, however. He did not have the right to will the house to you. I very much doubt if he would have done so in any case. It would have gone to my mother. It is her home, after all.' Alain Lemarchand's voice was now back to coldness, his dark eyes icy. 'Property in France is divided, *mademoiselle*. That is the law. At the time of your father's death, therefore, the house belonged to my mother, to you and to me.'

'I see.' Jenna bit into her lip and looked away. 'So the house will be sold and the money divided between us.'

'There is also land,' he rasped, looking at her irritably. 'However, there is no need for any of it to be sold. I have signed over my share to my mother. I am expecting you to do the same.'

CHAPTER TWO

THE cool expectation left Jenna speechless for a minute and then she glared up at him, her fair hair framing an angry face.

'Perhaps you can tell me why you imagine I would even think of doing such a thing?'

'It is the honourable thing to do.' He looked down at her steadily. 'There is a modicum of gentleness in your eyes and I presume that you are young enough to feel compassion. My mother has been happy there for fifteen years. It is her home.'

For a second Jenna stared back at him, anger mounting steadily. During much of that time *she* had been moving constantly, school friends, teachers and happy times discarded until she felt like a fugitive. Her soft blue eyes hardened as they had never done before in her life and she met his gaze head-on. It was time his mother felt the same kind of distress, the same feeling of being rootless; after all, that woman had stolen her father away.

'I have no intention whatever of signing away my inheritance,' she informed him coldly.

He had been watching the expression that crossed her face and now his own face closed to a sheet of ice.

'I do not exactly expect you to give your share away, *mademoiselle*. I am prepared to buy your share.'

'Let me get this straight, Monsieur Lemarchand,' Jenna said briskly, fighting down her own feelings before his renewed antagonism. 'Your mother bought you out and with that money you are willing to buy me out?'

'My mother did no such thing!' he informed her with aggressive force. 'I signed my share away gladly for no payment whatever.'

'Surely you don't expect the same kind of generosity from me? It is, after all, *your* mother.'

'It is what your father would have wished.'

'Really? I can hardly be expected to know that, can I? I haven't had a father for sixteen years. I can't even picture his face. He left us for a glamorous Frenchwoman and he never even sent me a card in all that time.'

His eyes narrowed thoughtfully and to her surprise and confusion he suddenly sat beside her on the settee, turning to her and looking at her closely, his gaze roaming over her flushed and beautiful face.

'You have been hurt in your childhood,' he stated quietly. 'Perhaps you do not really understand.'

'I understand! I've understood for years.' She drew back, rejecting this warmth that was so obviously designed to undermine her determination. Maybe that was how he got his own way? She had to protect herself and she would! 'My father found another woman who appealed to him more. He obviously found a ready-made son too.'

'Now you have found me also. Is it not astonishing to suddenly acquire a stepbrother?'

'Fascinating!' Jenna snapped, drawing further back. 'Save yourself the waste of so much expertise, *monsieur*. I will not sign over my share to your mother and I will not sell to you. I will instruct my solicitor to sell to any interested party.' She suddenly looked up at him with a slight smile, very bitter. 'I may even buy the whole thing myself if the price is right.'

'You expect me to accommodate you in that?' He stood and stared down at her. 'In the normal course of events these things take months. If you are to be awkward then my mother will not know where she stands for a good deal of time.'

'Neither did I, *monsieur*,' Jenna stated quietly. 'I was a child and unable to understand why he rejected me. I understand now, though, and it seems to me that I have no need whatever to rush into anything. Your mother will not be waiting for sixteen years, after all.'

For a second he looked exasperated and then he murmured something in his own language and suddenly drew her to her feet, his hands gripping hers, steadying her and comforting. He might not have meant to be comforting, but she felt a flood of warmth; energy passed from his fingers to hers like a life-force and Jenna didn't know what to say. Meeting him had rocked her safe little world; even his letter had done that.

'Come to France and meet my mother,' he suggested softly, his gaze on their joined hands. He looked up, pinning her with dark eyes. 'You are not giving us a chance. You judge without evidence.'

'I collected evidence long ago.' Jenna looked away and pulled free, motioning towards the door. She would not let this stranger get near her. She had built a safe world where nothing hurt, and she intended to stay in it. 'I think you should go, Monsieur Lemarchand. This can all be dealt with by solicitors.'

'We do not need solicitors for every tiny detail,' he pointed out exasperatedly. 'We will see enough of them as it is. I came to see you to create some warmth between all of us.'

'And how did you find me?' Jenna suddenly asked, remembering her own unease at this—and Glyn's suspicions.

'Private detectives,' he said in an offhand tone that infuriated her.

'Private detectives? How *dare* you have me investigated, followed around?' Jenna glared at him, her cheeks burning hot, and she was pleased to see that he looked satisfyingly startled at her temper.

Before he could answer, the doorbell rang, and after one more astonished glance at Jenna's furious face he strode out of the room to answer it, leaving her struggling with odd feelings. Damn him! He enraged her, but he made her feel guilty. He had her all mixed up. He was even answering the door, *her* door! He was treating her as if he knew her, as if he cared what she thought, and she couldn't even get her face under control.

Before she had managed it, she heard Glyn's voice, and it seemed of the utmost importance that he did not begin to get to know the man who had come here and turned her small world upside-down so quickly.

'In here, Glyn!' she called out almost frantically, and Glyn came through to the sitting-room, his eyes intrigued. Close behind him followed Alain Lemarchand, looking more suspicious than intrigued, and Glyn said the very thing she had been praying for.

'Hello, darling. I just dropped by to see if you were managing.'

'I'm fine.' She smiled up at him, all her natural sweetness clearly on her face. She was another person—her lovely mouth smiling, her eyes softened—and Glyn obeyed an impulse that came quite unexpectedly—he bent to kiss her soundly. He almost never called her darling and he certainly never kissed her in public, but there was a feeling in the air that he couldn't understand. Jenna looked different, confused, more alive than usual. It suddenly seemed necessary to stake some claim openly.

'I will leave now, *mademoiselle*. However, as you must surely understand, this is not the end of the matter.'

Alain Lemarchand's voice cut into this tender little scene coldly and Jenna looked up at him, her cheeks flushing more wildly. He met her gaze with a certain amount of scepticism, looking very satisfied when she found herself unable to meet his eyes for long.

'I will write to you,' he promised rather threateningly.

'Should I know about this?' Glyn's training suddenly got the better of him, but Jenna had no time to reply—the Frenchman did that smartly.

'There is little to know, *monsieur*,' he said coolly. 'In fact there is nothing to know unless you are extremely well acquainted with Mademoiselle Bryant. It is family business.' He nodded politely at the astonished face that Glyn turned on him and moved to the door. 'I will see myself out.'

'Just a minute.' Glyn pushed his spectacles back on to his nose and frowned, sliding smoothly into his role of family defender. 'I'm Jenna's solicitor.'

'*Vraiment*?' Alain Lemarchand turned and regarded them both with ironic amusement. His lips quirked and his mind was very obviously on that kiss. 'The English have strange habits,' he mused sardonically. 'However, if you say you are her solicitor then I must believe you. I am her stepbrother. It is perhaps a closer relationship after all. *A bientôt*, Jenna.'

He smiled with malicious satisfaction into her red face and walked out.

'What was all that about?' For the first time ever, Glyn's unruffled demeanour seemed to be slipping. The intrigued look had changed to suspicion and a certain amount of acrimony. 'I may not yet be family, but I do know enough about you to know you don't have a stepbrother.'

'I thought so too,' Jenna murmured, trying to get her agitated breathing under control, quite sure that this was doing her no good at all when she had been told to go very carefully for a while. 'I've suddenly acquired a stepbrother, as he pointed out. My father married his mother. You were just bandying words with Alain Lemarchand.'

'Really?' Glyn sat down, his suspicious looks vanishing. 'I suppose you asked for identification?' he added seriously.

She felt suddenly quite piqued and definitely ready to snap. First Alain Lemarchand with his forceful manner and now Glyn with his everlasting questions. She really wanted a cup of tea and she knew perfectly well that Glyn would serve her up something that looked like brown shoe polish. For the first time ever she wished he would go and that Shirley would come back in.

'I didn't need identification,' she said bleakly. 'He didn't come to take anything away. He came to tell me I have a legacy.'

'Why come here? It could all have been taken care of without you bothering. That's what solicitors are for.'

He sounded a bit pompous, verging on Ned Clarke's manner. Jenna had never noticed the trait before, but she supposed he was being over-protective. After all, she needed protection right now. Something alien and dangerous had just left her house. It had got amazingly close to her too.

'Apparently he came because I'm so very young. He wanted to tell me off about not going to see my father before he died. My accident and stunned expression seemed to excuse me, however. Monsieur Lemarchand wants to tie up all our affairs with some speed.'

Glyn just glossed over the bit about her father's death with a wry little look. He found it hard to express sympathy and, in any case, he was more interested in legal matters.

'Then he can tie them up with the firm. Let me have the details and I'll pass them on to Ned Clarke.'

'Not yet.' Jenna leaned back and regarded the ceiling with a pleased little smile. 'I'm going to waste time. As much time as possible.'

She was finding some sort of bitter happiness in this. Let Alain Lemarchand's mother wait. Let her be unsure and worried. Her own mother had been unsure and worried and so had she. Besides, it seemed to be terribly important to get the better of one arrogant Frenchman. She didn't like the way he had moved in on her so quickly. He had to be kept well away from her and then defeated. Time was on her side. He had said that French law moved slowly; *she* was about to make this into a record case.

Nothing could move her and when Glyn came back later for dinner, armed with further arguments, he realised she was completely adamant. The house and land could just sit there and Monsieur Lemarchand's mother could sit wherever she was and wait. Glyn told her it was unreasonable, but she just didn't care. It seemed to her to be the nearest thing to rough justice that would ever present itself. Nothing could hurt her mother now and nothing could hurt her father even. It was the Lemarchand woman who would be hurting and probably fuming with impatience.

Besides, Alain Lemarchand had unsettled her. She couldn't get his face out of her mind, for one thing, and she felt embarrassed now about that burst of warm concern. It had been a trick and she had almost fallen for it. She still felt the power of those strong fingers, the protection that had seemed to swim around her. If she had simply gone straight to France when she had received his letter she would have fallen for it even more. She would have been at his mercy and she didn't suppose he had any such thing. It was better not to see him again. She could do without a powerful, handsome French stepbrother, especially one who had used private detectives to find her.

Ned Clarke didn't appreciate her views at all. Two weeks later she was summoned to his office. She still felt very tired and run down, but her excuse was neatly removed by Glyn when she pointed out that she didn't feel quite up to driving.

'Oh, I explained that to Ned. I'm driving you there and back,' he informed her. 'Ned's a bit concerned about this inheritance of yours. The French are notoriously slow about legal matters. He feels they need a prod.'

'It's only two weeks and I want things to be slow!' Jenna pointed out crossly. 'I've waited sixteen years to hear from my father and they can wait for as long as I can drag this thing out. We haven't even begun yet.'

'Things should be taken in hand,' Glyn stated firmly. 'Lemarchand might be up to anything.'

'He already played his hand and lost. According to him I should simply sign over my share to his mother.'

'*What*? You never told me that!' Glyn looked at her with a good deal of accusation. 'Look here, Jenna, he may be your stepbrother but you don't know him from Adam. For all you know he might be a very shady character.'

'No,' Jenna asserted firmly. 'A forceful character, but definitely not shady. He looked as if he could buy up this whole street of houses with the petty cash. He's not after money or anything like that. He feels his mother should be able to stay in the house she's been happy in.'

A wave of guilt washed over her which she angrily pushed aside. She hardly ever stopped thinking about Alain Lemarchand and each time he came into her mind this guilt came too. He still seemed so real, so close that she could feel his disapproval, and somehow she felt he was using will-power from a long way off. It was most irritating.

'It's easy enough to look wealthy,' Glyn pointed out impatiently. 'Confidence tricksters do it all the time. He came to wangle your legacy from you and you refused. I'm proud of you. It proves my case that he hasn't been in touch again. He lost and he's given up. I expect he felt it was all over when he saw me and realised our relationship. Now you have to act. In any case, Ned's a bit peeved so you'd better go in and see him. He is the senior partner, after all.'

And was pressurising Glyn! Jenna could tell that. Maybe she should act? Perhaps his mother was just sitting there in the house knowing that this could take ages and more than content to wait; after all, what was she losing? Certainly Alain Lemarchand had not been in touch, unless you counted thought-waves. This was quite ridiculous, after all, merely a legal transaction. Let Ned Clarke deal with it and then they would be out of her life. It was no use being vindictive if she was merely upsetting herself.

She collected her coat and moved to the door with Glyn. She still felt a bit wobbly on her legs and she knew too that she could do with a holiday. It was a bit scary to cut an artery and they had cancelled their Italian holiday at once. School had started, but Mrs Constantine was aware that Jenna was not ready to go back yet.

'Leg all right?' Glyn asked vaguely as he settled her into his car. He didn't have much patience with any kind of illness, she already knew that, and he was a terrible patient himself. In the winter he had gone down with a slight burst of influenza and anyone would have thought it was the plague.

'Leg's fine.' He didn't even seem to notice her wry humour. His mind was on other things, and she suddenly found herself back again thinking of Alain Lemarchand and his expression when she had moved forward.

'*Mon Dieu*! You are ill!'

She could still hear his voice. How would he have reacted if she had really been ill? Would he have tried to make her give up her share of this house and land? For someone she had met only once he had had a remarkable impact on her. She had only just been out of hospital then. If she saw him now it would be quite different, of course. She would not feel so defenceless.

'I wonder what he's really like?' Jenna was a bit startled to find she had spoken the thought out loud.

'Who?' Glyn glanced across at her and she had to look away and pretend indifference.

'My stepbrother.' It didn't sound so bad if she said it like that—family—no threat to Glyn's ego. She was becoming a trifle uneasy at Glyn's bossiness.

'A rogue,' he snapped sarcastically. 'Mark my words. Not that it matters. You won't be seeing him again.'

It sounded like an order and Jenna was surprised at the feeling of alarm it gave her, as if she was trapped, unable to make her own decisions.

'I may have to go to France,' she managed hastily, not really meaning it but feeling the need to assert herself. Since her accident Glyn had very subtly changed. She had been vulnerable—long days indoors, and then the need of transport as she didn't feel up to driving. It had all put her in Glyn's power somehow and she no longer had that feeling of independence she had fought so hard to gain. She sometimes felt stifled.

'If a trip to France is necessary, I'll go to represent you,' Glyn stated firmly. 'No need for you to go at all. I'm more of a match for Lemarchand.'

He wasn't. Jenna looked at him secretly and knew he would be no match for Alain Lemarchand at all. Also, it was one more step towards being subdued. If it was necessary to go to France she would go herself. Not that it would be at all necessary, she reassured herself as she felt a sudden burst of fright.

Ned Clarke informed her otherwise. She sat opposite him as he leaned back in his seat and observed her through gold-rimmed spectacles, and she still felt uneasy with this man.

'Your legacy is going to be a trouble,' he informed her coldly, his spectacles glinting. 'I've been making enquiries on your behalf and I'm astounded—astounded!'

If anyone else had had this odd habit of repeating himself, Jenna would have laughed, but with Ned Clarke it wasn't at all laughable. It was rather sinister. He had a lot of peculiar habits, one of them being to stare hard at you with steely eyes.

'Er—what kind of trouble?'

He stared at her as if she already knew and was simply being obstructive. Apparently, though, her innocent looks convinced him, because he leaned back again and gave a weary sigh.

'I've been dealing with your affairs for some considerable time, Jenna,' he pointed out, as if it had been a dreadful chore wished on him by some unseen and malevolent spirit. 'Your mother left your well-being in my hands.'

This time it was Jenna who was astounded. She had never heard such nonsense. Her mother had died a very short time ago, in reality, and Jenna had been more than capable of dealing with her own well-being. She had a job, a house and enough money to live fairly well; in fact she had been quite surprised at the amount of money her mother had left her. Jenna's shocked looks must have reached some deep core of humility in Ned Clarke. He flushed uneasily.

'What I mean is—she explained your circumstances quite openly and asked that if anything happened to her I would keep an eye on your affairs.'

'Thank you. I did realise that,' Jenna said quietly, still looking at him warily. 'We were strangers here then, and in a way I'm a stranger here still. After my father left we only had each other and—and we moved a lot.'

'So I understood. Of course, after a divorce it is often. . . Be that as it may, when your mother decided to divorce her husband——'

'She didn't have a lot of choice!' Jenna stated hotly. 'After all, he walked out on us.'

'That is not what she told me,' he said primly. 'Your father was an artist, as I believe you know. He went to France to paint and stayed there for longer than she thought necessary. Your mother started proceedings. She called it desertion and I often suspected that there was another man.'

'*What*?' Jenna struggled to her feet, but he waved her back to her seat.

'All verifiable if you wish to bother. This of course is not the reason for this little chat.'

Little chat! She felt as if she were in the middle of a minefield. Her father had left them for a woman in France. Now he was telling her that her mother had divorced her father because there was another man in her life. What other man? She had no memory of one.

'Monsieur Lemarchand is being quite obstructive, to my mind,' he went on grimly. 'In the normal course of events these things take time under French law, and they're likely to take even longer in this case because he refuses to make any move whatever until you are actually there—in France.'

'Why?' Jenna found herself almost whispering. She had been secure, certain of her facts, her life built on the reality of the past, and now things were all tilted, wavering, with a man she did not know issuing orders that would take her towards a place she had no desire to visit. She also felt as if she were sitting in front of a bespectacled lunatic who was making things up as he went along.

'He insists that you meet his mother and discuss things—reasonably.'

'Then he can just go on waiting,' Jenna stated with a firmness she certainly didn't feel. Alarm was racing over her skin. 'It suits me to delay.'

'Please be sensible.' The gold-rimmed spectacles were glinting at her again and this time angrily. 'Your father was a very reputable artist, a fact you may not have realised. In France he was well known and his work sought eagerly. This house and land are not all that is left behind. There must be other things, valuable things, not least paintings. He did not live in an empty house, and some of those possessions are yours. You must go and look, claim them, be there at any discussions. You own part of his estate.'

'Is—is that why Monsieur Lemarchand wants me to go?'

'Not at all. I imagine he wants to put some pressure on you. It had puzzled me originally, but after a quick word with Glyn as you came into the offices I now see he wants to pressurise you into following his wishes and signing the house over.'

And that was quick work. She had only told Glyn about it on the way here. The feeling of being manoeuvred came back with a rush and she had the urgent desire to get out of this stuffy office fast. People seemed to be arranging her life without even consulting her.

'He won't be able to pressurise me, Mr Clarke. I've already told him how I feel.'

'Certainly he will not,' Ned Clarke stated with pursed lips. 'Glyn will go with you and take care of your affairs.'

It was said with such certainty, as if she were a slightly incapable old lady, and Jenna found anger mounting to add to her feeling of things being taken out of her hands.

'I can take care of my own affairs, thank you.'

'I really think not. If you should decide to go. . .'

Svengali! That was what he was like. She knew now why she had always disliked him. Ned Clarke was one of those men who manipulated people. Well, not her!

'I am going, Mr Clarke.' Quite suddenly, her mind was made up. It was now or never. When she married Glyn she would inherit this odd man too in a way. She had wild visions of being obliged to invite him to dinner every night. He might want to see her grocery list and cross a few things off. 'I'll make my own arrangements. I shall go alone.'

'You're not capable,' he said disapprovingly.

'Do you mean mentally or physically? I always thought my intelligence was more than adequate.' She had the satisfaction of seeing Mr Clarke's face redden with embarrassment. At least it got her out of his office without more lecturing, and when Glyn presented himself rather smugly she told him smartly that she intended to go to France and she intended to go alone. Nothing would move her.

Somehow or other she had been manoeuvred into being a poor weak female, bordering on the edge of dimwittedness. She was more than capable of taking matters into her own hands. In any case, she needed a break. She certainly needed a break from Glyn, and if she never saw Mr Edmund Clarke again it would be too soon. She had an open-ended arrangement at school. She was to return when she felt up to it. She could spare the time for France.

Alain took her phone call with remarkable calm, his voice on the phone almost making her decide not to go. It sounded like another person. The original answer had been from a woman and the French had baffled her. All Jenna had been able to do was say, 'Monsieur Lemarchand, *s'il vous plaît*.' It brought forth a flood of French until Jenna stopped it with a rather desperate admission that she did not speak the language.

'You are English, *mademoiselle*?'

'Yes. I—I would like to speak to Monsieur Lemarchand, if that's possible.'

There was the sound of a busy office and she suddenly thought he would not speak to her. When he came on the phone almost instantly, she found it impossible to speak.

'*Vous désirez, mademoiselle*?' The deep voice was at once familiar and yet strange and Jenna was utterly at a loss as to how to answer. Tingles ran down her spine and her mouth went quite dry. The silence held for a while and then she heard a low laugh that seemed to trace itself right down her spine too. 'Mademoiselle Bryant, is it not? I recognise your silence.'

'I—I had to call you because. . .'

'Because you have decided to come to France and investigate your inheritance,' he finished for her. '*Eh bien*, I will meet you. Give me the time of your flight and I will arrange everything else.'

'I haven't actually said anything at all about coming to France,' Jenna managed in self-defence.

'Then why are you wasting my valuable time, *mademoiselle*? You are checking up on me, finding out if I really exist? I assure you that I do. If that is all I will say goodbye to you.'

'Wait!' He sounded as if he was about to simply replace the phone and go, and Jenna had steeled herself for this. She felt she couldn't do it again and she wasn't about to crawl back to tell Ned Clarke so and have him volunteer Glyn for the job. 'I do want to come to France. My solicitor says you're being—being obstructive.'

'So you are coming to sort me out? I expected it. Tell me your travel arrangements.'

'I haven't made any yet.'

She could just hear the silence filling with exasperation, but when he answered he was quite in control of his temper and his voice.

'Very well. I will make the arrangements for you. There is a flight in the morning. I will meet it and take you back with me.'

'I don't know if I can get the flight and I don't want to go anywhere with you. I had thought a hotel. . .'

'Then you had thought irrationally. As our affairs are somewhat entwined at the moment, naturally I will collect you and take care of you. As to the flight, I will book you on to it and ring you back when the arrangement is secure.'

'But. . .'

'Give me your number and do not go out for the next half-hour.' When she gave him the number he just rang off and left her staring at the phone. What was she doing? She had stubbornly defied both her solicitor and Glyn and here she was letting a complete stranger dictate terms to her. When the phone rang again she was still sitting there staring at it.

He read out her time of departure, time of arrival and flight number, advising her to write it all down as if she was a half-wit, and she was glad he wasn't there to see her face as she scrabbled for a pen and paper.

'The flight is paid for and I will meet you on arrival,' he finished. 'Do not change your mind, *mademoiselle*,' he added softly.

'I won't!' There was an underlying sound of laughter in his voice. He clearly thought he had won and it annoyed her. 'I have every intention of coming to sort things out.'

'Ah! You are bringing your solicitor friend. I did not book his seat. *Quel dommage*!'

'I'm not bringing anyone at all and, as to the seat, I'll pay for mine as soon as I see you.' He was laughing as he rang off, and she could almost feel his satisfaction. It alarmed her all over again.

As Jenna waited to be collected in Paris she began to think that this was not a good idea after all. It was something she had been determined not to do right from the first, and yet here she was, waiting for Alain Lemarchand, butterflies in her stomach threatening to make her feel sick.

It was only two days ago that she had decided to come and now, as she stood there in the spring sunshine, she could hardly believe she had allowed this to happen. It was the result of being determined not to be manoeuvred into things she didn't want to do, and yet she most certainly didn't want to do this.

She had great misgivings. She should perhaps have brought Glyn after all. He had been very annoyed at being left behind. He had pointed out all the disadvantages. She could not speak French, she was quite weak and, worse still, she was a woman. That last seemed to be a disadvantage she was born with. Both Glyn and his boss had made that quite clear with no words needed.

All that faded from her mind as she saw Alain coming towards her. Tall, lean-hipped and broad-shouldered, he seemed to tower over everyone else, and once again there was that air of casual elegance about him that had her looking him over with her heart in her mouth.

Even before he got to her she was mesmerised, the dark eyes holding her with complete ease, and she had to bring herself quickly back to the present to do what she had planned and set matters on an even footing straight away.

'My fare. I asked how much and this is it.' She dived into her bag and held out the necessary money, and at least it stopped him in his tracks, although it left him looking down at her with less than pleasure.

'I anger quite easily,' he murmured quietly, taking her cases and ignoring her outstretched hand and the money it held. 'Also I am accustomed to courtesy and react badly when it is not present. Normally I expect to be addressed with a polite "*Bonjour*". Greetings that begin with money being thrust into my hand do not amuse me.'

'Very well. I apologise, *monsieur*. I'll begin again. *Bonjour*, here is your money.'

She looked up at him defiantly and his cold stare turned to reluctant amusement, the dark eyes holding hers flaring with that same recognition she had seen before. If he thought she was going to be a nice little stepsister he could think again! His lips quirked at her expression and he turned away.

'Just follow me, Jenna. My car is not too far off. We will fight in private. It is what families do, *n'est-ce pas*?'

'I'm not family.' He had taken not more than two strides and yet he was leaving her behind. She was still very shaky and the journey, short as it had been, had tired her, but he hadn't seemed to notice. He noticed then and stopped abruptly.

'Even now you are not better? Be still. I will help you.' He signalled imperiously and a porter seemed to materialise from nowhere to take the two cases, and that left Alain free to deal with Jenna. He took her arm as he had done at the house, his hand under her elbow, her weight against him, and she was powerless to alter the facts.

'Two small cases only?' he enquired. 'You do not, then, intend to stay for very long?'

'It—it's only a business trip, after all,' Jenna said breathlessly.

'Perhaps we will change your mind.'

'We? Is your mother here?'

'Here? In Paris? As yet, no. She will arrive tonight or perhaps in the morning. She has been taking a small holiday. We have cousins in Provence and she is there at the moment. I told her of your arrival and naturally she is anxious to meet you.'

'Why?'

Jenna began to feel panic-stricken and, again—manoeuvred.

'Why? She is your stepmother. Surely that is obvious? Naturally too you will wish to see your inheritance. *Alors*! Let us go.'

They had arrived outside and her cases were deposited in a long silver car that Jenna thought must be a foreign make, probably Italian. She didn't have the chance to look. The porter was tipped, Alain was in the driving seat, and she was being swept away by a complete stranger to a house she didn't know at all, far away from anyone who would help her. It scared her, but as she glanced secretly across at the face she had never forgotten for one moment she realised she was more excited than scared. Somehow it was like an adventure.

His dark eyes met hers as if he felt her surreptitious

appraisal, and she found herself at the receiving end of that long, sardonic smile.

'*Tout va bien*,' he assured her in amusement. 'I do not kidnap young females, even for financial reward, and also, if you were to disappear without trace, it would be years, I suspect, before my mother had her home to herself. Think about that when you are secretly summing me up. I told you that the law does not forget you. If you disappeared it most certainly would not. I must make quite sure that you remain healthy and visible.'

'I'm not scared,' Jenna lied. In fact she was, a little. She felt extremely vulnerable at the side of this powerful man. Belatedly, she wished that Glyn were here with her. The trapped feeling must have been because she had been indoors for a long time. Glyn was reliable and right now she needed him. She might not be able to cope with Alain Lemarchand.

CHAPTER THREE

THE house was beautiful and the sight of it silenced Jenna utterly. It was about twenty-five miles west of Paris, set in several acres of grounds with tall trees, and it was not at all what she had expected. She hadn't given much thought to what the house that her father had left would be like, but she had not gained the impression that it was anything like this. Certainly she had not envisaged this grand and elegant residence.

It was white, three storeys high, the lower windows arched, as was the front door. A double flight of shallow steps led to the door, which was flanked by stone pots of flowers now brilliant with spring colours.

'It's beautiful!'

As the car swept up the drive the words were almost torn from Jenna in awe and Alain glanced at her quickly.

'It is certainly pleasing to see and comfortable to live in. There are nine bedrooms, many with bathrooms *en suite*. Of course it has been altered and modernised inside to a great extent, but outside it remains as it was, a Louis-Phillippe property and therefore beautifully proportioned.'

Jenna didn't know what a Louis-Phillippe property was, but she was completely entranced. She remembered saying that she might very well buy out the others and live in the property herself. One thing was sure: she couldn't afford it, because she hadn't even imagined anything so grand.

Her father must have been really successful to have bought this house and had it altered. So close to Paris, it would be expensive, and Alain must indeed be successful in his work too if he could afford simply to give his share away to his mother.

It annoyed her to think he had imagined she would do the same. Even a third-share of this house would represent a fortune to most people. It would be interesting to know what he was proposing to offer her to sell out. And anyway, what about the furnishings and the pictures? She looked across at Alain rather grimly. He hadn't mentioned that at all. Maybe he *was* a confidence trickster. The thought was vaguely disappointing and that feeling alone annoyed her more than ever.

'We arrive.' The car swept up to the front of the house and Alain stopped. Almost instantly Jenna could hear bird-song and for a moment she just sat there, drinking in the atmosphere. It was so wonderful that she didn't really want to get out of the car. She would have been quite content simply to stare at the house for hours, and she was still sitting there when Alain opened her door and bent to look in at her.

'You are either tired or entranced,' he commented. 'If it is merely enchantment I suggest you allow me to show you around. First, however, we will have coffee.'

A man came from the house as Jenna was getting out of the car and she was quite impressed. He was some sort of a manservant, because above his dark trousers and over his white shirt he had the sort of striped waistcoat she had imagined such people would wear—normally only in films, though, especially as this particular waistcoat was striped in black and subdued gold.

'There has been a call, *monsieur*,' he announced, taking the luggage and casting one interested look at Jenna with dark eyes that widened perceptibly as he noticed her ash-blonde hair, almost silvery in the sunlight. '*Madame* is on her way back. She will be here very shortly, probably within the hour.'

'*Très bien*, Jules. That is good timing, *n'est-ce pas*? Meanwhile, this is Mademoiselle Bryant. We will take coffee at once and then I intend to show her over the house. I will pray there is not too much dust around.'

'I guarantee there is little, *monsieur.*' Jules gave a very controlled smile. Apparently he was quite used to the caustic humour that Alain seemed to favour. 'Your father was a very talented man, *mademoiselle*,' he added quietly. 'He will be missed.'

Jenna just nodded. For the life of her she couldn't say the expected thing and it hurt with surprising depth that this man had known her father when she herself had not known him at all. The hurt tightened her lips and she absolutely refused to look at Alain.

She wished she hadn't come. She wished she hadn't seen this house where her father had lived. Obviously Alain had been so sure she would come that he had even warned the servants. This man had known exactly who she was and had taken the trouble to speak in English. Glyn had been quite right after all. A solicitor could have done everything. There was absolutely no need for her to be in France. She was being manoeuvred here too and it would be even more difficult.

As if he was attuned to her thoughts Alain made no move to help her as she went towards the house. Jules had already disappeared indoors and Alain merely matched his pace to hers. Maybe he was giving her time to look around, but now she didn't want to. The old bitterness was back with a vengeance and she kept her face averted.

He suddenly muttered in exasperation and took her arm, making short work of the steps.

'*Ciel*! You are a stubborn child!'

His observation embarrassed her out of silence and she struggled belatedly.

'I'm not in any way a child!'

'In years, perhaps not, *mademoiselle*. In behaviour—I reserve judgement. You are obviously tired and I imagine that nothing would make you admit it. What happened to you exactly in this accident?'

'I lost a lot of blood. The glass just touched an artery.'

He led her into the hall with a shining expanse of parquet floor in front of her, his hand still on her arm.

'You should not have come alone. Had I realised what had happened I would not have allowed it.' His possessive tone annoyed her.

'*You* precipitated this trip!' She shrugged his hand away and glared up at him, her pale face a trifle flushed, and he looked down at her with sardonic interest.

'Stubborn, ungracious and of uncertain temper,' he observed drily. 'Traits inherited from your mother, I would imagine. Certainly Russell was a gentle and even-tempered man.'

'You didn't know my mother!' Jenna's voice rose, her blue eyes wide and angry, and one dark brow rose in surprise as he watched her.

'Happily, I did not,' he agreed cynically. 'Come along. Coffee will be served in the long drawing-room and, if you are to battle with me, may I remind you that it is to be in private. There are servants in this house and they are not accustomed to war-like behaviour.'

He turned towards a tall white door and opened it, waiting with very studied politeness for her to approach, his eyes roaming over her sardonically until she blushed to the roots of her hair.

'I should never have come here,' she muttered as she drew level with him. 'Glyn was quite right. He should have come on my behalf.'

'Ah! Your amorous legal adviser? We do not need that particular addition to the family.'

'I am not family!' Jenna snapped. 'And Glyn is not amorous. As a matter of fact,' she added hotly, 'I'm going to marry him very soon.'

'And he has no amorous inclinations? I find that very

peculiar, but then the English are cold-blooded, are they not? It is perhaps to be expected.'

'You have no right to speak to me like this!' Jenna stood in the doorway and glared up at him and he simply took her arm and drew her into the room, closing the door firmly.

'But normally, *ma chère*, I would not. However, I have observed that you are war-like. Scratch me and I bite.'

'I will have as little to do with you as possible, Monsieur Lemarchand. I most certainly will not be scratching you.'

Jenna stood as firmly as possible and tried to make her voice cold and hard. It wasn't easy. She really didn't want to battle with him. For one thing, she was almost entirely at his mercy, even to the point of getting out of here and back to Paris and her plane home. For another, it was upsetting.

About to motion her to a seat, he spun round and looked down into her face, seeing far too much. He saw the anger, but he also saw the very raw vulnerability and the tiredness. It didn't seem to ease his cynicism.

'You will not scratch me? We will see,' he murmured, making her blush wildly at the innuendo. He suddenly grasped her chin and tilted her reluctant face. 'You will call me Alain and I will call you Jenna. I have ventured into the use of your name several times but you have not returned the compliment. Now you will remember. I am your stepbrother. My name is Alain.'

'Will you please stop claiming a relationship that I consider does not exist?' Jenna said stubbornly. 'I don't know you. I'll be here for only a little while and I prefer to stick to formality.'

'I will not have my mother upset.' For a second, his hand tightened painfully, but almost at once he relaxed his grip, his thumb running along her jawline. 'As to not knowing me, I think we have fitted into a peculiar relationship very quickly. Sometimes knowledge comes in a flash, sometimes one does not have to see someone for weeks at a time. We knew each other on sight, did we not?'

'I expect it's because you're my stepbrother,' Jenna said sarcastically. She jerked her face free and sat down, putting as much distance as possible between herself and those hard, warm fingers without actually running away, although she would have liked to run away right at that moment. She had no idea what he was up to. She glanced up defiantly and he was watching her intently, his dark eyes searching her flushed face.

'I do not want to know you at all, Monsieur Lemarchand,' she stated firmly. 'We both know why I'm here and it is not to claim some long-lost family.'

'Perhaps I do not want to know you either, *mademoiselle*,' he rasped. 'However, I appear to be stuck with it.'

He turned away impatiently and Jules came in at that moment, bringing coffee on a silver tray, and the conversation had to end, to Jenna's great relief. There was an atmosphere that was almost crackling in this room and she was sure that Jules would notice, but apparently he did not. He nodded to her and placed the tray on a low table beside her and left as quietly as he had entered.

Automatically, Jenna began to serve the coffee. The china was wonderful—delicate and costly, like pieces from a collector's hoard. Her eyes moved over the room too. The elegance was there, the wealth, the furniture exactly what this room needed, and she was sure that the whole house would be the same—perfect.

'You enjoy good things, do you not?'

When she glanced up, Alain was watching her, noticing her approval, the rather wistful looks she was casting around. It made her bristle.

'You mean I'm greedy?'

'Perhaps you are, although I did not even imply it.' He accepted his coffee and regarded her quizzically. 'You have what is called, I believe, a large chip on your shoulder. Tell me about it. I already know you feel that you were deserted by Russell.'

'I don't just feel it, *monsieur*. It is a fact, a fact I've lived with. It's significant that you sit here in this house, so comfortably, calling my father by his first name while I haven't seen him since I was eight.'

His amused speculation died very quickly at that.

'The choice was yours, I think. You gave me to understand that even if you had not had your accident you would almost certainly not have come to France to see him at the end.'

'At the end? What about all the years? Let me tell you, Monsieur Lemarchand, that, while you and your mother were living here in the lap of luxury with my father, my own mother was forced to move constantly to cheaper accommodation. I had to discard my friends, my teachers and my life over and over in order to move. You seem so settled here. You fit so beautifully into the surroundings. It must have been a wrench to give some of it up, but you had a choice; I never had a choice.'

He looked at her steadily for a moment and then his hard expression softened considerably.

'No. You did not have a choice. First you were a little girl and then you were a teenager with long silvery-fair hair and long, slender legs. Choice was taken from you until finally it was too late.'

It was an odd thing to say and Jenna didn't challenge him. It was almost uncanny the way he had painted a picture of her teenage appearance. She was beginning to think he had a way of entering her thoughts and her memory, because she had looked like that when they had made their final move—tall, slender, leggy.

Her mother had stated then that it would probably not be necessary to move again, but she had always shied off from friendships—so many of them had been lost before.

It hadn't seemed to be worth while, not worth the hurt and upset.

'Well, now perhaps you'll understand why I have no intention of giving up anything,' Jenna stated. 'I've given up too many things in the past and I intend to hang on to every penny that the sale of this house fetches. You'll have to fit yourself into other surroundings, as I had to do so often.'

'Actually, I can fit myself into most surroundings,' Alain informed her. He was smiling to himself—some private joke—and it made her anger rise swiftly, but he went on before she could take him to task. 'You are very changeable, Jenna, adapting to different circumstances like a camouflage. You are angry, vulnerable, gentle, fierce, with such bewildering speed that I find it fascinating. Is this because of the strange life your mother forced on you or is it a natural trait of character?'

'I don't find this at all amusing,' Jenna snapped. 'I'm here strictly for business and being dissected does not appeal to me at all. If you want my real character I'll tell you. I can fight for whatever I want and I'm hard as nails.'

'You do not lie well, *petite*. Give it up.'

'Will you kindly not call me that?' Jenna jumped up, almost spilling her coffee, making a hasty grab for the delicate cup and amusing him even more. Of course, he could afford to be amused. They were probably hers anyway.

'It is merely an endearment. You are family.'

'I'm an enemy, here on business,' Jenna informed him fiercely. 'Let's get down to the business now. I haven't all the time in the world. I work, if you remember?'

'Of course. You are a strait-laced schoolteacher. I have not forgotten. As to the business: first you will meet my mother. She is anxious to see you.'

'I have no intention of meeting her,' Jenna began, but

he too stood and looked towards the long windows as a car came speedily to the house.

'Unless you intend to hide behind a door, it is too late. My mother has just arrived and I would say from the look of her she is all set to greet you as a long-lost child.'

'I—I'm not. . .'

'But you are,' he assured her. He was suddenly sombre, tilting her face as the dark eyes looked straight into her own. 'I know you are hurting, but do not judge too hastily. My mother is hurting too. For now she feels that her life is over. Your own life has just begun, remember that.'

He turned to the door and then looked back.

'Her English is not too good. Most English people have some small amount of French. I assume you do too?'

'I do not, *monsieur*. I very carefully refrained from learning French.'

His eyes narrowed at this bitterness, but he simply left the room, and Jenna had the feeling that she had been as ungracious as he appeared to think. She didn't understand this man at all. He seemed to be a mixture of kindness and mockery, but it didn't matter very much. She was here to fight him. Inside she knew her mother would have wanted this. She had no intention of being accepted by this family.

She looked down hastily at her own appearance. Until now she hadn't given it much thought. She had been swept along by Alain since her plane landed and now she was about to meet the woman whose glamour had brought her father to France, who had driven him to deserting his own wife and child.

French women were chic, well groomed, and if all the magazines were to be believed they were almost invariably beautiful. She caught sight of herself in a long gilt mirror and smoothed her fair hair. She was wearing a mulberry-coloured suit with a straight skirt and a short jacket. It had travelled well and the colour emphasised her astonishing fairness. She would just about do, although she wished she had been able to wear high heels. If *madame* was like her son then she would be as tall as a tree.

High heels were out for now, though; she felt shaky enough as it was. She turned to the door, almost shivering with nerves as she heard the rapid flow of French from the hall and knew that now she was about to meet the woman she had unconsciously hated for the whole of her life.

She could hardly believe what she actually saw. As the door opened, Alain ushered in a small dark woman, his hand on her shoulder, and Jenna's expectations collapsed like a deflated balloon. She just stared uncomprehendingly. *This* was the woman who had lured her father away? This small, uninteresting woman with short greying hair and a plain face?

Oh, she had the chic that seemed to be the birthright of all French women, but she had nothing else at all, unless it was the rather fine dark eyes, the only thing she had in common with her tall and impressive son.

'Jenna!'

Alain's sharp command had her jerking her head up from her almost frantic study of his mother, and she realised that her fixed stare was embarrassing the woman a great deal. She hadn't meant to do so. It was all too late now and with the woman here, right in front of her, it seemed so pointless to feel animosity. It was almost impossible anyhow because this was not the glamorous and deadly creature of her imagination.

'My mother,' Alain announced forcefully, his eyes on Jenna as if he was willing her not to sink back into her rather threatening stance. It must certainly have looked like that, she realised. 'And this is Jenna,' he added, looking swiftly at his mother. 'Russell's daughter,' he tacked softly on at the end.

Neither woman spoke and Alain gave them both a wry look before urging his mother further into the room. Movement seemed to bring a bit of life to the woman, who regarded Jenna with rather sad eyes as she came forward uneasily.

'I have wanted to meet you for such a long time,' she began hesitantly. 'My—my English is not too good, you understand, but I would like to be able to talk to you for a while.'

With Alain's dark eyes on her quite threateningly, Jenna had to pull herself together fast.

'Thank you, *madame*. I'm afraid I don't speak French at all and in any case I will not be here for long, but *madame*. . .'

She wasn't quite sure what she was going to say. She felt completely shattered by the woman who watched her. Alain intervened, however.

'My mother's name is Marguerite. I'm sure she wants you to extend the same warmth to her that you extend to me by using my first name.'

Wickedly sardonic, he was even taking this opportunity to reissue his orders, and Jenna looked like a trapped rabbit.

'I—I. . . If Madame. . .'

'If you prefer formality, then of course we must defer to you,' Alain said silkily. 'Naturally, though, my mother's name is Bryant, like yours.'

Jenna flinched. She just couldn't help it, and Marguerite looked at her son as if he had gone quite mad.

'Alain!'

'It is as well to get these things over with at once,' Alain said coldly.

'Then forgive me, Jenna. I think we need a moment to recover. I—I'll see to my luggage. Jules may not have. . .'

There were tears in her eyes that Jenna did not miss,

and as the door closed she turned her blue eyes on Alain. They were blazing with fury.

'You unfeeling pig!' she denounced hotly.

It earned her a menacing look as he stepped forward.

'And what are you, Mademoiselle Bryant? You deliberately fixed my mother with a glassy stare and frightened her out of her wits. I told you that she felt her life was ended. I do not wish to see it actually end here in this room as you attempt to stun her with blue-eyed hatred!'

'I wasn't doing any such thing! She simply took me by surprise. She's nothing at all as I imagined.'

The confession seemed to remove a bit of his fury, but he did not relax very much.

'What exactly did you expect, a siren?'

'My—my mother was beautiful and yet. . .'

'And yet your father preferred Marguerite. I understand perfectly well that your mother too was blonde and beautiful.'

'Then why. . .?'

'Why, *mademoiselle*? Perhaps it is a good question to ask. Looks are not everything. Character is more lasting. You are astonishingly fair and beautiful. It does not make you attractive.'

'I wouldn't want to be attractive to someone like you,' Jenna blurted out, driven to defending herself.

'Perhaps not. To whom are you attractive though, *mademoiselle*? Even the man you propose to marry is not amorous, upon your own admission.'

'You're quite a hateful man,' Jenna choked out, turning away from the cold, taunting eyes.

'It was not my intention. You are making things difficult for all of us with your bitterness.' He spun her towards him, his hand against her face as she turned. 'You are young enough, intelligent enough to cast it off. I have already told you that you are judging without evidence.'

He suddenly let her go, turning away impatiently and pressing a bell.

'Jules will guide you to your room. If my mother feels the need to recover then perhaps you do too. Though I warn you,' he added menacingly, pointing one long brown finger at her, 'if you persist in upsetting her I will not hesitate to punish you even though I know how this hurts. Go and—and wash your face or something,' he finished in exasperation as Jules came into the room.

She didn't exactly flee—she wasn't physically capable of it—but it felt like that, and the stairs were an almighty pest, stretching as they did almost endlessly. Jules paced beside her and said nothing at all, imagining no doubt that she was a poor little orphan. She gritted her teeth and made it to her room in spite of everything.

The warmth that Alain had shown her from time to time had quite gone now and she knew he would continue to be an enemy. It was necessary to get this over as soon as possible and then leave. She could stay in Paris tonight, or even get a late flight back.

She was summoned down in exactly fifteen minutes and this time she was more prepared. Now it would be business. There was the house to sell, the things to divide. If they wanted to make an offer she would listen and think it over. She made it down into the long drawing-room with a sort of grim look on her face that Alain noted with a frown.

Marguerite was already there and she too seemed to have pulled herself together because she took charge of the conversation at once.

'I was sorry to hear of your accident,' she began. 'I know it meant that you didn't see your father but——'

'I may very well not have come in any case, *madame*.' Jenna saw no reason to hide the truth and no reason to pretend that this was some sort of family gathering. 'I thought about it and decided that it would have been very awkward both for my father and everyone else, not least myself. I didn't know him and only at the end did he wish to know me.'

'But, *ma chère*. . .!' Marguerite looked shocked, her eyes turning to Alain for some sort of confirmation, but Jenna was not waiting at all.

'As far as I am concerned, *madame*, the sooner we get our affairs sorted out the better. I was quite content to let the whole matter be dealt with by solicitors, but your son seemed to be insisting upon my presence here. Well, here I am. Now if we could get down to the sale of this house and the contents. . .? I understand that you now own two thirds of it?'

'Alain?' Marguerite looked at her son in utter bewilderment and he simply sat back and smiled. 'Alain? What is all this?'

'I would think—a misunderstanding,' he said smoothly, his eyes on Jenna's determined face. 'How it has come about I cannot think, but of course we must set things right.' He smiled at Jenna like an amused tiger. 'This is not the house your father left, *mademoiselle*. You are part-owner of a farmhouse in the Dordogne, the south-west of France. It is completely restored, set in about ten acres of land, rather isolated but with fine views. It is quite charming. My mother loves it.

'At the moment, property is considerably cheaper here in France than in England. In English terms I would say that the property that Russell left is worth about ninety to a hundred thousand pounds. This house is worth at least three-quarters of a million pounds. Unfortunately, this house is mine.'

While he had been talking like an estate agent, getting his full value out of the situation, the full embarrassment of it had been dawning on Jenna. It wasn't only the words she had just used to Marguerite. She remembered the things she had said since she came into this house. How could she have been so stupid? Her father could not possibly have owned a house like this, nor could he have owned half the things in it. It was the home of a very wealthy man, a man she had recognised as wealthy the moment she had seen him. Alain Lemarchand.

And he had let her go rambling on. Oh, she could now understand his amusement when she had snapped out her thoughts. It was just the sort of thing that would amuse a man like that. She was unable to think what to do, trembling and pale with embarrassment and shame. All she could do was stumble from the room and get out of their sight as quickly as possible.

'Jenna!'

She just ignored Alain's voice and ran up the stairs to her room, ignoring the way it made her dizzy. She would leave. She would leave at once, call a taxi and get back to Paris. After this, Glyn could come. He could come and argue to his heart's content. She had thought he was manoeuvring her. She had never been manoeuvred into a situation like this before. She was shaking with shock and humiliation.

As she got to the top of the stairs she could hear Marguerite arguing with Alain. She couldn't tell what the words were, but she was grateful that he was being detained. She flung herself into her room and began to pack frantically, wanting to cry with rage and shame.

She was churned up inside, unable to see beyond this moment. It hurt very, very badly, but what hurt most was the awful feeling of having let herself down. She had played a part that was alien to her nature and she had not played it well at all. She had tried to be hard and grasping, tried to deal with this in a sophisticated, detached manner. It was not in her character to be any of those things and she felt cheap and foolish, like a wicked child caught stealing.

Alain came in without even knocking and she turned on him with furious hurt.

'If you would have the patience to wait, *monsieur*, I intend to go home. You may do as you wish with the legacy because I'll never come back to this hateful country.'

'You will,' he said quietly. 'Do not keep this up, Jenna. You're hurting, and I have added to it with my stupidity. I am truly sorry. Forgive me?'

She turned her face away, embarrassment bringing her to the brink of tears.

'You're not sorry. You made a fool of me and thoroughly enjoyed doing it! Well, I hope you're satisfied, because now you can deal with Glyn!'

'I did not set out to make a fool of you. At first I could not believe you thought this was the house and later. . . well, I enjoyed listening to you going on about it. *Dieu*! I have made a fool of *myself*. If I were not so big my mother would place me across her knee and spank me. I am not at all sure that she will ever speak to me again.'

'She's on my side?' Jenna turned to look at him, unaware that tears had escaped on to her cheeks, and he grimaced ruefully.

'Most definitely. I would think if you looked carefully you would find that most people are.' He looked at her firmly. 'Come downstairs and we will talk together.'

'No! I'm not talking to anyone at all and I certainly don't want to talk to you ever again.' She turned back to her packing, her hands trembling almost uncontrollably. His regrets were certainly short-lived. One apology and then back to orders. It had not eased her embarrassment.

'Jenna! Be sensible! You have worn yourself out with this.' He sounded accusing and she glared at him wildly.

'And it's your fault!'

'I admit it.' He shrugged irritably. 'I will admit to almost anything if you will calm down and talk to my mother. I want this thing settled. I want to see you both happy.'

'Don't make me laugh,' she raged, packing frantically. 'I'm nothing at all to you except an unwelcome visitor.'

'You are not unwelcome. You are very important.'

'Rubbish!' She swung to face him angrily, her pale cheeks now flushed to wild apricot, her breasts rising and falling with bottled-in emotion, annoyance, embarrassment and a feeling of having been manipulated into a situation where she had behaved like an ill-bred lunatic.

His eyes ran over her from the wild disorder of her pale hair to the agitated beating of the pulse in her throat and the smooth rounded thrust of her breasts, and he looked at her angrily.

'I wanted you to come here to face your past, also to make a sort of peace both for yourself and my mother. I admit to yielding to the temptation of allowing you to think this house was your father's, but my thoughts have not all been selfish. If you could tell me what I'm getting out of this turmoil I would be pleased to hear it.'

Offhand she couldn't think of anything. What did he need, after all? He was so obviously wealthy. It might be that he was speaking the truth, but before she could answer footsteps sounded along the passage, and they both faced the door as his mother came reluctantly in.

'My dear child. . .' she began hesitantly. 'You must try to forgive us. Please do not go away.'

'We will join you downstairs and this time we may have some sort of rational discussion,' Alain said firmly, taking matters into his own hands.

'Oh, I'm so glad. I think I'll order English tea.' Marguerite left, and Alain looked at Jenna with challenge in his eyes.

'You can see that she wants you here. Whatever you think of us, you must know that. My mother is incapable of any sort of subterfuge. You will stay?'

'I don't seem to have a lot of choice,' Jenna admitted, looking ruefully at the mess she had made of her own clothes. 'I really don't want to hurt your mother.'

'I never believed that you did. I understand you much more than you think. Leave this chaos,' he added impatiently. 'A maid will sort it out.'

'What will she think?' Jenna looked back over her shoulder a little anxiously as she was led firmly to the door.

'That the English are mad,' he murmured derisively. 'Do not worry. It is well known. Why do you think we pander to the peculiarities of your countrymen? We are an understanding people.'

He looked across at her and she hastily looked away. She seemed to have acquired a lot of peculiarities herself. He had almost made her feel at ease, but her embarrassment was not something she could laugh about. She felt very shaky and she was glad he held her arm. The stairs had an alarming tendency to swim up to her.

On the way down the stairs they passed a maid and he issued very firm orders without stopping for one second.

'Unpack for *mademoiselle, s'il vous plaît*, and press her clothes.'

'*Oui, monsieur.*' She gave Jenna a startled look and disappeared, and Jenna thought of the mess she had made of her things. Well, if that didn't confirm the insanity of the English nothing would. At this moment it was difficult to recall how quiet, calm and determined she had been. It all seemed like a long time ago, but actually it was only this morning. Of course, that had been in England!

CHAPTER FOUR

MARGUERITE looked a trifle anxiously at Jenna as she came back into the room.

'I am sorry, Jenna,' she began, but Alain stopped her at once.

'No. *I* am sorry! I think perhaps that I am at least partly forgiven.'

'Then let us get on with the business that must be discussed.'

She motioned Jenna to a seat and it was clear that her initial diffidence was now controlled. She took over the serving of the tea and cakes and Jenna had the opportunity to study her surreptitiously.

Marguerite was not exactly a motherly woman, but she was in some way comfortable. Not by any stretch of the imagination could she be called beautiful and it was doubtful if she ever had been, but she was undeniably attractive. She was wearing a mixture of clothes that should not have gone very well together, but they did.

She had a poise about her that spoke of some sort of inner peace and Jenna's mind went back to her own mother—the beauty, the restless energy, the quick, sharp voice. All things that had combined to make Jenna the quiet sort of person she was. There had been no room for competition with her mother and Jenna had never wanted to try to offer any resistance to the relentless drive that kept her mother going.

It was true that this woman was the exact opposite. Had that fact alone drawn her father to Marguerite Lemarchand——? No, it was Marguerite Bryant now and had been for over fifteen years. The dark eyes looked up and saw Jenna's interest.

'You must see the house tomorrow,' she stated quietly.

'No.' Jenna looked down, her eyes on the cup she held tightly. 'Coming here was a mistake. Tomorrow I'll go home. I—I didn't come in any good frame of mind, *madame*, and now I'm rather ashamed of myself. For many years I've hated you and it seems so—pointless.' She looked up, her blue eyes wide and rather vulnerable as she smiled faintly. 'You're not even the person I hated. I just imagined you all wrongly.'

'What else could you do?' Marguerite's voice was warm when Jenna had expected another burst of either anger or distress. 'I took your father away, *n'est-ce pas*? In your mind I was a scarlet woman and could be nothing else. You did not know me. You did not even know Russell.'

'Well, it's too late now,' Jenna sighed. 'It was always too late, I expect.' She pulled herself up sharply from being mournful. 'I'll leave all this to—to Alain and to my solicitor. I—I think it best if you keep the house, *madame*. I know my solicitor is going to be annoyed by all this, but. . . If I could perhaps have a picture my father painted?'

'You will see the house, child. You will see where he lived and worked and then we will discuss the future,' Marguerite said with a finality that left Jenna astonished. She hadn't imagined that this woman could be at all assertive, but she was being exactly that now, and Alain had so far said nothing at all.

Jenna stole a look at him and he was watching her intently, in every way intent. She had called him by his name—a thing she had so far refused to do. She was also following his wishes, handing over things to him and to his mother, so why was he looking so explosive?

'It's not necessary, *madame*,' Jenna began, switching her eyes back to Marguerite with a great effort.

'It is very necessary,' Alain cut in harshly. He got up and went to stand by the tall, ornate fireplace where a fire had now been lit for the cooler evening to come. 'You did not know Russell. For a short time at least you should be able to trace some of his life and it is all there in the Dordogne. Tomorrow I will drive you down there. My mother is going home in any case and we will go with her.'

'I couldn't stay at the house. . .'

He looked as if he was fighting the desire to glare at her, but his mother's eyes were on both of them and he answered quietly enough.

'Then I will stay with you and drive you back here. It is a relatively easy run down if we start early in the morning. We will be back here by nightfall. Maybe by then you will have changed your mind about things.'

'I won't. I'm sorry, but I just don't want to go.' Jenna looked back at him, her lip caught between her teeth, and he frowned down on her, preparing to lay down the law severely by the look of him.

'Leave it, Alain,' Marguerite said quietly. 'This has been quite a shock—for both of us—and Jenna does not look at all well.'

She didn't feel well either. It had been more of a shock than she could have anticipated. There seemed to be nothing now to hang the rest of her life on, and Alain had a very disturbing effect on her. She had behaved quite out of character just to get the better of him. Things had certainly changed since she had received his letter.

As Marguerite left the room for a moment to answer a phone call, Jenna looked up at Alain. He wasn't looking at her. He was staring into the fire rather grimly and she had to take her courage firmly in hand.

'I'd like to go home tomorrow,' she said softly, earning herself an instant retaliation.

'So nicely said,' he grated. 'Just like a little girl. "May I go home, please?" Who is stopping you, *ma chère*? I will drive you to the airport. I will help you to run away.'

'I'm not running away!' It was a protest that gained her a derisive smile.

'No? I believe you are. You are proposing to send your solicitor friend to deal with things. You are about to tell him to attempt to fight things out with me. There is no need. State the price and I will pay it.'

'I'm not bothered about the price,' Jenna protested, moving in agitation. 'Now that I've met her I——'

'You find her not the threat you had imagined. This I know too. You are still fleeing from the past, though, behaving like a trained poodle, moving on rapidly as your mother taught you. You are programmed to run!'

'I'm not!'

Jenna jumped up, agitated even more when he moved over to her. His strong hands spanned her delicate shoulders and tightened.

'You are. You cannot face what must be faced. You cannot look into Russell's life and risk finding your own unacceptable.' He suddenly relaxed his tight grip and turned away. 'You imagine it will not linger in your mind like a lost tune? You will come back again and you will search.'

'I will not come back. You know nothing about me.'

Jenna's face was very pale and he looked at her and then looked away.

'I knew Russell,' he stated quietly. 'Finally, you will wish to know everything.'

'*Nobody* is going to trap me!' Jenna said shakily, and he turned narrowed eyes on her.

'A strange expression. Will you feel trapped when you marry this lawyer of yours?'

Jenna knew she would feel trapped—she had known for quite a few days—but she was not about to tell Alain Lemarchand that, and she was just gathering her thoughts to answer when Marguerite called from the hall.

'Alain? Claudine is on the phone and she would like a word with you.' He walked out and Jenna sat down abruptly, shaken and bewildered. Did things like this happen? Was this what she had felt as soon as she had seen him—a man who would interfere with her life? He was making her think more deeply about herself than she had ever done.

She was white and trembling when Marguerite walked back into the room, looking quite alarmed when her eyes fell on Jenna's pale face.

'Jenna! You look quite dreadful!' She walked across and took Jenna's limp hand. 'Your pulse is fast. Perhaps I should send for the doctor?'

'No! No, *madame*, please! I just feel a little faint. Today I've rather put myself under a strain. I'm supposed to take care for a while. It was a very unfortunate accident. If—if I could have my dinner in my room tonight I'll be perfectly well tomorrow.'

'Of course, *ma chère*. Let me help you to your room. I will see that you are not disturbed until dinner and then you shall have a tray. You must stay in bed by all means.'

She helped Jenna out and they could both hear Alain on the phone in another room. She wanted to be out of his sight very quickly and she leaned on Marguerite willingly to get up the stairs as fast as possible.

A doctor? What she needed was a psychiatrist! Alain Lemarchand was trying to organise her life. Tomorrow she would go home as early as possible and she would never see him again. She would settle back into her safe routine and forget this time.

It didn't work out quite like that. Jenna slept badly, waking with a throbbing pain in her head, and it took a great effort to swing both her feet from the bed and sit on the edge. She felt quite weak and she was still sitting there, staring disconsolately around the room, when Marguerite knocked and walked in.

'Oh, you are awake? If you are up so bright and early we will be able to set off in very good time.' Her voice died away when she saw the strain on Jenna's face and she came round the bed, her eyes racing over Jenna's pale face. 'You poor child! Why, you look like a ghost. Get back into bed. I will send for the doctor at once.'

'There really is no need, *madame*,' Jenna said quickly, thinking that another day here would just about finish her off. Right at this moment she would have given anything for a sight of Shirley and endured her fussing with pleasure.

'There is every need. You must rest, but first, the doctor!'

'*Madame*, I am going back to England today. This is very unfortunate, but it isn't a very long journey. I can manage and when I get home there is a good neighbour who will——'

'*Qu'est-ce qu'il y a*?' Alain had just walked into the room and stood in the doorway with a frown on his face that promised trouble, and his mother appealed to him instantly.

'Jenna is not well, Alain, but she refuses to have a doctor. She says she is going back to England——'

'Call Moinet!' he ordered, walking completely into the room, ignoring Jenna's blushes as she sat there in her nightie, which wasn't particularly revealing but which felt like it at the moment.

He looked extremely annoyed and she was thankful to see Marguerite hurry out to obey. Moinet would probably be the chauffeur in this grand household. A lift to Paris at least.

'Thank you. If you could go out, I can get dressed and be ready when he comes. I have two cases to pack.'

'Do you?' he enquired grimly. 'And just where do you think you are going with these cases, *mademoiselle*?'

'Why, home. You just called your chauffeur and——'

'Moinet is the doctor. He will be here before very long. He is efficient and, in any case, we know him well.'

'How dare you just—just overrule everything I say?' Jenna stormed. 'I want no doctor. I can rest at home and that's where I'm going.'

'You came to France to settle the matter of the inheritance,' he pointed out, glaring at her. 'It will be settled before you go. I am not particularly patient about unfinished business and I mean to see my mother happy and settled before you leave.'

'I've *told* you she can deal with my solicitor!' Jenna snapped. 'Whatever you want to do—do it. I don't want to see the house or anything—I just want to go home.'

'Leaving my mother to feel that she has cheated you? *Pas question*! You will follow every suggestion she makes because the only way you can get back to Paris is on two feet and I doubt your ability to even walk across this room.'

'*Do* you?'

Jenna stood up defiantly, her head flung back proudly. There was no way he was going to trap her here to solve his problems. The Lemarchands were nothing to do with her.

Her head swam and she swayed dizzily.

'Little fool!' He was upon her in two strides and swept her up into his arms. 'You are going nowhere at all,' he assured her grimly, looking down at her as he sat her on the bed, her legs on top of the sheets, and she was too busy trying to make sure she didn't faint to consider how she looked.

'I would say you have two choices,' he rasped, frowning down at her. 'You may rest here for as long as Moinet orders or you may rest in hospital.'

'I—I feel quite sick.'

'No, you do not.' His hand came hard and warm to her nape, tilting her head forward as he sat beside her. 'Breathe deeply and relax,' he ordered.

In a few seconds she felt better and raised her head, her eyes enormous in her pale face. He was looking at her so intently that she closed her eyes again.

'I feel all right now,' she managed shakily.

'You do not. You are not moving from here, *madem-*

oiselle.' His hand was still massaging her nape and all the fear and tension seemed to be draining away, leaving her drowsy.

'I'll have the doctor,' she sighed tremulously. She had a great temptation to rest against him, but he stood with a swift movement that was all anger and sarcasm.

'That last has never been in any doubt. He will be already on his way. You may be with us unwillingly, but you are certainly with us for the time being.'

He whipped back the covers and moved her into bed as if she were a doll, watching her for a second and then turning away.

'I can't just stay here!' Jenna looked at him anxiously and he spun back to stare at her, anger on his face until he saw how pale and shaken she looked.

'Why?' He came and sat on the bed at her side again. 'You are not with strangers.'

'Of course I am. Until yesterday I had never seen your mother. Even what I imagined isn't true. I've seen you very briefly in England and now here. What are you both but strangers?'

'You may have never seen us before, but you are no stranger,' he said softly. 'We have heard of you for many years. The lovely fair-haired Jenna. The lost child. When we finally get to the house I will show you something and maybe you will change your mind about many things.'

'Nothing can alter facts,' Jenna said shakily. 'You're not family.' She rested her head back on the pillows and looked at him a bit desperately. She was in no state to argue with someone so powerful.

'For myself, I do not wish to be family,' he murmured, his glance sweeping over her pale face. 'I wish instead that you should know where you belong. There are roots here that were laid down for you. It will heal the past.'

'You mean you're going to help even if it kills me?' Jenna asked crossly, and he suddenly smiled, the dark eyes dancing.

'You are perfectly safe. Did I not tell you that I must keep you well and visible for my own protection?' Unexpectedly he reached across and ran his fingers down her smooth cheek. 'Keep on looking like that and Moinet will insist that you stay here indefinitely so that he can look after you. You look very vulnerable. I believe it is called "pale and interesting".' He stood and moved to the door. 'Whatever the doctor orders you will do, *mademoiselle*,' he finished firmly, no sign of humour left. 'We will consider the next move when you are well.'

He walked out and Jenna looked at the closed door. She should be feeling trapped, but somehow she didn't. She had no desire whatever to stay and become enmeshed in the affairs of Alain Lemarchand and his mother, but he had simply gathered her in imperiously as if he were in charge of her life. It was probably frightening, but right now she only felt weak and tired, grateful that somebody was taking charge. She could sort anything out when she was better.

The doctor was middle-aged and gentle. He was very interested in Jenna's accident and stayed quite a long time. His English was almost perfect and he told her he had treated several English people. Marguerite stayed too, and the whole thing proved to be quite a little occasion. His final words were that she needed a nice long holiday after a few days in bed. Marguerite surprised her by nodding wryly and making a small grimace. 'I told you so' was written across her face.

Alain came in as the doctor's car left the house and he stood at the foot of the bed and regarded her sternly.

'Two days in bed and then a nice relaxing holiday,' he reminded her.

'Well, I was planning to go to Italy when I had my accident,' Jenna mused, trying to take matters back into her own shaky hands. 'I suppose we could reinstate that if Glyn can get the time off.'

'Your holiday will be in the south-west of France,

mademoiselle,' Alain said forcefully. 'When you are well enough you are going to the Dordogne. You are going to eat well, sleep for long hours and look at your inheritance.'

'You know perfectly well that you can't order me about,' Jenna informed him. She was already feeling a bit better and she felt quite amused at this cool domination, especially as she was not going to pay any attention to it.

'I probably can.' He looked at her quizzically. 'At the moment you are weak and shaken. I can take advantage of it. In any case,' he added sardonically, 'it is better to be in the Dordogne with your stepmother than in Italy with a man who feels no passion for you.'

'You have no idea what Glyn feels!' Jenna's cheeks flushed with embarrassment and he slanted her a look of dark-eyed amusement.

'You assured me that he had no amorous intentions. What a waste of Italy. Wait until some man who wants you takes you there.'

'I don't like this conversation, if you don't mind,' Jenna said primly, wanting him to stop at all costs. 'It's not very proper and if I were on my feet you wouldn't say things like that.'

'Of course I would,' he assured her ironically, his dark eyes gleaming with malicious amusement. 'I am French, *mademoiselle*. We are not a cold-blooded race. We are more down-to-earth. I am merely pointing out the disadvantages of a romantic trip without romance.' He suddenly laughed, the sarcasm dying away. 'In any case, I am well content. I am getting my own way as usual. My mother is already planning the trip happily.'

'I—I won't be trapped!' Jenna said with sudden anxiety. 'It's cruel of you to try to force me into this family. I can't change my mind about the name Lemarchand as suddenly as this.'

'Then change your mind slowly,' he urged seriously.

'As to trapping you, are you not already trapped by the past? Your hatred of my mother disappeared as you looked at her. Already the walls are falling. Face the past and you may find it is not what you thought at all. That is not trapping you, Jenna. It is freeing you.'

He walked out and Jenna relaxed against the pillows. She knew he was right about his mother, but she also knew she would never forgive her father. If she went to the Dordogne she would be facing a life that had gone on without her, a life that had not for one minute taken her into consideration. She knew what Alain had said about her being the lost child, but even he did not know how lost she had been. There was no easy recovery from that. There was only forgetting it and getting on with her present life.

Her present life was Glyn and their plans for the future. It was true that they were vague plans, but they were there all the same. She felt flustered when she remembered what Alain had said about going to Italy. Glyn did want her. He wanted to marry her. It was all happening comfortably just as she wished.

She didn't want passion. Somebody like Alain Lemarchand would have the sort of passion that would scare any normal woman. So many expressions crossed his dark face and even when he was amused there was a sort of hard sensuality about him.

Jenna turned fretfully on her pillows. Sensuality was a word she had read like any other English word. Until now it had meant nothing at all, but now she really knew what it meant. She could do without it. She was comfortable with Glyn and she wanted nothing more than that. Alain could keep his comments to himself.

She was to be in bed for three days at the doctor's insistence and she never even saw Alain. It gave her an incredibly guilty feeling, as if she was a nuisance and should be away from here and not causing so much trouble. By the end of the second day she had it firmly fixed in her head that Alain was simply ignoring the fact that she was here, and as this was his house she couldn't make her mind up whether this was discourteous or a great relief.

She saw a lot of Marguerite and slowly learned to relax in her presence. Again this brought guilt piling in on her head, because she felt the beginnings of a great liking for the woman who had stolen her father away. Her mother would not have found this amusing.

'Alain will be home in the morning,' Marguerite observed as she came to bid Jenna goodnight after her second day in bed. 'I am pleased to say that you look much better. It will please Alain too. You had us quite worried.'

'Isn't he here? I—I thought. . .'

'You thought he had decided to stop being so tyrannical?' Marguerite's lips quirked at Jenna's expression. 'Oh, do not be embarrassed, Jenna. Alain is a very powerful man—like his father—but unlike his father he has more than his share of kindness. Still, if he had not been called away he would have been up here, no doubt, demanding to see progress. Tomorrow, however, he returns.'

'I'll be up by then,' Jenna stated hastily.

'Not until the day after. Doctor's orders.' Marguerite left after this little show of determination and Jenna sank back against the pillows, realising that the thought of Alain coming back was a little worrying. He would start to pressurise her again and she didn't really want to go to the Dordogne at all. Somehow she was afraid that she would discover things she was better not knowing.

Next morning Jenna got up anyway and she was walking slowly round the garden when Alain pulled up in front of the house. He did not see her at all as he got out of the car and Jenna had the chance to observe him without the dark eyes pinning her quizzically. He looked tired and slightly irritated. The long, carved lips were set in a tight line and the straight black brows were screwed up in a frown.

Something or someone had annoyed him and instantly she assumed it was because he was landed with her here in his house. It brought a painful flush to her cheeks and at that moment he looked up and saw her.

'I imagined you had been ordered to bed for three full days.' He stopped and stared at her rather alarmingly, his eyes running over her from head to foot. 'You are not too good at obeying orders, *mademoiselle*.'

'I felt all right. I'm taking some gentle exercise.' She said it with a sort of breathless defiance, and his eyes narrowed.

'And you are feeling guilty about it?'

'Not at all! I'm in charge of my own affairs, Monsieur Lemarchand.'

'Then why the flushed face?' He walked slowly over to her, his jacket slung over his shoulder, his briefcase in his hand, and when he was towering over her she found it difficult to maintain her attitude.

'I suppose I was feeling a bit guilty about being here,' she confessed in a burst of honesty that she instantly wished back. 'I—I mean. . .you look tired and. . .'

'And you immediately assumed that you had outstayed your welcome and I would be thinking to myself, "*Mon Dieu*, now I have to face that idiotic English girl." If you recall, I was the one who insisted that you stay.'

'I wouldn't have stayed if I hadn't felt so ill, and now that I'm better I'll go home if you can get me to Paris, Monsieur Lemarchand.'

He made a wry grimace and turned her to the house.

'Do not irritate me further,' he murmured. 'I have not had a good day; in fact I have not had two good days. I need a shower and then I need some peace and quiet, a little sanity perhaps. I also need to be called Alain. You try my patience, Jenna.'

'When I'm back in England——' she started sharply, but her voice petered out as he interrupted harshly.

'It may very well be weeks before you are back in England. French law works slowly but surely. As you have not even seen your inheritance yet very little progress has been made.'

'Then Glyn can come out and see to things.'

'My mother's affairs and your personal problems are nothing to do with any English solicitor. It is a family matter.'

'I'm not family.'

'Repetition will not alter things,' he informed her caustically.

He took her arm and led her indoors whether she wanted to go or not and Jenna said nothing more. He had taken over her affairs again, picked them up as if he had never been away, and she could do nothing about it unless she began to create a great fuss. That would only upset Marguerite and now she didn't want that at all. She was comfortable with Alain's mother; there was an inexplicable safety about her, a permanence.

'I have silenced you?' Alain looked down at her as they came into the hall. 'I am not quite sure how I did that. I must try to remember.' Without warning his derisive expression faded. He suddenly pushed his fist against her chin in a gently bantering way, his attitude softened. 'Take this to my study, there's a good girl. I shall not be civilised until I have showered.'

He suddenly dropped a quick kiss on her startled lips and then bounded off up the stairs, and Jenna was left with his briefcase in her hand, her expression stunned. She went slowly along to the door she knew led into his study, and now it was Jenna's brow that was creased in a frown.

She did not want to be mixed up with them. She did not want a family. She didn't even want French friends. Friends always had to be left behind and, in any case, she didn't want to hear about her father's life in France. Alain was wrong about that. There were no roots prepared for her here and she would not come again to search if she left now. She would leave tomorrow. She would phone Glyn and then concoct some excuse—school, for instance. Her mind was quite made up.

Having her mind made up had done very little good, Jenna mused next day as they sped down the motorway that led to the Dordogne. Alain had walked all over her excuses and her call to Glyn had left her quite at Alain's mercy—not that he knew it.

Because of the strange happenings since she had arrived, Jenna had almost forgotten her original reason for this trip. She had remembered all too well as she spoke to Glyn.

'Exactly what I expected—what I tried to shield you from,' he said with very grim satisfaction. 'You're not equipped to deal with things like this, Jenna.'

All this he had concluded from a rather wistful statement that she was missing him. He knew nothing of the other facts and, as he continued relentlessly, Jenna was pleased she had not told him. Apparently, missing Glyn showed how incompetent she was, and she had a rather annoying vision of him going into see Ned Clarke and passing on the information with a sceptical look, a sort of 'what will these women get up to next?' expression.

After that she had been at pains to assure him she could cope very well and was about to go to see her inheritance. When he asked if he should fly out her answer had been a firm and uncompromising 'No!' but now, as she glanced at Alain, she was not too sure if she had been wise. At the moment her life seemed to be like an obstacle race, side-stepping men who were determined to deal with her affairs.

'Not too long now,' Alain remarked. 'As it is Friday afternoon I am at your disposal until Sunday night. If you decide to stay in the Dordogne with my mother I will stay too until Sunday evening. It will give you time to make up your mind about staying longer.'

Jenna bit her lip in vexation. She had made it quite plain that she was not about to stay here at all, but Alain had outmanoeuvred her with ease. In the first place he had been in to his office and delayed their departure until after lunch. In the second place he was behaving as if this was a holiday—a welcome break from his busy life—and if she wanted to go back it would mean he would go back too. She would feel like a spoiled child insisting that she wanted to go home. She didn't even know what he did to earn so much money, anyhow!

They were running through thickly forested country, and tension began to mount in the car. None of it was coming from Alain. Jenna knew without being told that Marguerite was finding this difficult; each mile had added to her own anxiety, and Alain's mother was feeling many anxieties too.

For Jenna, it was a barrier she had never expected to have to cross, this venture into her father's past. She was afraid, afraid of making a fool of herself, afraid that past bitterness would sweep over her and make her behave badly. She suspected that Alain's mother was anxious for the same reason, and Jenna could not help glancing across at her sympathetically. It was brave of this woman to bring a resentful and hostile stranger into the place that had been her home.

Jenna could not help feeling hostility, but none of it was directed at Marguerite. It was all centred on a man who was now dead, a man who had cast her aside long ago. Any dregs of left-over resentment were directed at Alain Lemarchand, the man who had forced her into this, the man who had forced both of them into it. She was determined that Marguerite would not suffer for it, and she clamped down on her growing fears. Whatever awaited her at the end of this journey she would face. She had faced worse, after all.

She looked up and found Alain's eyes on her, the dark gaze studying her through the driving mirror. She had been placed in the back for comfort, or so he said, but Jenna had not been fooled. Alain had not allowed her to be where he would have to talk to her. His only remarks had been addressed to his mother, who sat beside him. He had said nothing to Jenna except his recent comment that they were almost there. Now he was studying her, waiting for reactions, waiting for a scene. Well, there would not be one.

She looked abruptly away and turned her eyes to the small villages they sped through, pretty places with interesting-looking shops. Well away from the motorway now, each new place quickly gave way to further forest and, just as Jenna was beginning to be lulled into a strange peace by the dappled sunlight of the place, the soothing green of nature, the car turned on to a narrow road and began to climb steadily.

She didn't have to be told that they would be arriving within seconds; Marguerite's tight shoulders told her that and Alain's lips tightened too as the tension in the car reached him. He shot a threatening look at Jenna, but she was now too worried to be annoyed. It was here now, the place where Russell Bryant had lived happily while she had run with her mother from place to place. They had all lived happily here. Her eyes glazed with tears, but she blinked them away. One more hurdle, one *last* hurdle and the past could go back where it belonged.

CHAPTER FIVE

THE forest thinned out and then was left behind. It was not seconds but many minutes before they climbed to the top of the road and came out into fresher country, and the farm was there, nestling in the late sunshine, the fading light turning its stone, creeper-clad walls to amber. It was long and low with dormer windows in the red-tiled roof. A barn was attached on the left side and the whole place stood in the centre of a stone courtyard.

To each side were gardens brilliantly blooming with the flowers of spring. The white paintwork of the house glittered in the light, its long windows shining, and Jenna had to stifle a bitter cry. She did not need to be told that they had been happy here, the three of them. It was welcoming, warm, as home should be. Even Marguerite's tight shoulders relaxed and, as he slowed the car and finally brought it to a halt before the house, Alain made a sound of deep satisfaction.

'At last!'

Jenna didn't know if he meant that they had finally arrived after a long journey or if he was reliving his youth here, claiming his past again. One thing she did know, however—there were no roots here for her, nothing to find. *Their* roots were here! All that had happened to Jenna was that an old, painful wound had reopened. The bitterness rushed back and overwhelmed her. She could not even imagine her father here. She had no idea what he looked like. She had *forgotten*!

She suddenly realised that they were both staring at her, watching the expressions chase each other across her face. They probably thought she was resentful and sullen.

Certainly Alain seemed to think that. He was looking at her with frowning concentration.

Before he could speak the door opened and a young girl appeared, smiling at them.

'I have tidied up and laid the fire for evening, *madame*. It has been chilly these past few nights. Mademoiselle Rabier phoned, *monsieur*,' she added with a sidelong look at Alain. 'She will phone later.'

Alain just nodded and Marguerite smiled at the girl. 'Thank you, Marie. You had better go home now before it gets too late. I'll see you tomorrow.'

The girl left after a curious look at Jenna and another swift glance at Alain. Jenna could tell that she was wondering who this newcomer was. It looked as if she would have news for Mademoiselle Rabier when she saw her. Maybe Mademoiselle Rabier was the Claudine who had phoned when they were in Paris? Jenna was not too interested. She had enough to worry about and the greatest worry was how to make herself step inside this house.

Alain collected the luggage and made it plain that he was not about to coax her. He expected good behaviour and his rather grim glance in her direction did more to motivate her into action than any coaxing. It said quite plainly, there will be trouble, *mademoiselle*, and Jenna followed Marguerite into the house that had been home to her father for all those years.

It was modern. That quite startled her and at least it gave Marguerite a starting point for conversation.

'This place was very run down when we bought it,' she said, looking round lovingly. 'There was a huge fireplace, very much the original thing, but quite ugly. One thing we are rather good at in France is making unusual and beautiful fireplaces. As you can see, this brings the whole room together.'

The fireplace in question was set into a huge thick wall that partly divided the main room. When lit it would warm both sides and make the atmosphere cosy. There was a copper canopy over it and Alain bent and put a light to the logs that were already there.

'Pictures are better than explanations,' he said sardonically. He then ignored both of them, walking to the stairs that curved down into the room and taking the luggage up.

Jenna tried to ignore him too, although whenever he was near the air seemed to be crackling between them. She looked at the old narrow beams that stretched across the ceiling, at the white-painted walls and the brightly coloured furniture, comfortable chairs and the mellow, shining wood of tables and bookcases. She could see the pictures that graced the walls, but her mind refused to acknowledge them. Perhaps they were her father's, perhaps not, but she was not going to ask.

'The kitchen is through here,' Marguerite said quietly, leading her into another room. 'We eat in here too. There is nothing grand as there is in Alain's house, but it is comfortable.'

It was. The white equipment built into the walls was all modern, but it was softened by the glowing pine of the table and chairs, the sloping, beamed ceiling and the brightly coloured pots and pans. The table was set for a meal, fresh flowers in the centre, and Jenna saw tears spring to Marguerite's eyes. She was remembering and finding it painful, and Jenna's gentle nature came to her rescue.

'It's lovely. Can I see upstairs?'

'Of course!' Marguerite pulled herself together and led the way back into the room they had first entered. By now the fire was crackling merrily, the flames beginning to soar up the chimney and cast brightness on the walls. Jenna hastily looked away and followed Marguerite up the curved stairs and on to a long landing.

'All the bedrooms are to the front of the house. It means that they all have the same good view. The bathroom is at the end, facing the back and the woods, but in any case each room has a small bathroom *en suite*. At one time we contemplated incorporating the barn, but Russell needed a studio and it was ideal. In any case, we have never needed much room. Three bedrooms are enough. I expect Alain has given you this one. It is the guest room.'

She opened a door and Jenna could see that her cases were already there. It was a lovely room, again with a sloping roof. The bed faced the window that looked out over miles of countryside and it seemed that everything in the room was white, from the white, frilled curtains to the dainty white duvet cover and pillow case all edged with broderie anglaise. There was a bright red chair in the corner, though—a soft, comfortable chair with silken cushions—another, smaller, matching one by the bed, and Jenna was quite entranced.

'How beautiful!' For a moment she was too filled with emotion to say more and Marguerite glanced at her quickly, patting her arm.

'I will start the meal. Stay here and unpack, Jenna. Both of us need a few moments alone to come to terms with things. Try to understand, I beg you.'

She was gone before Jenna could answer, the door softly closed behind her, and Jenna went to the window, looking out over the fields to the forest in the distance. In due season there would be poppies in those fields, bright red reminders of other years. The trees close to the house would shed their blossom and fruit would come, apples and cherries to be gathered and join the carefully stored pots in the bright kitchen. So many years of memories. How poor her own memories seemed at the side of this. She knelt down by the low window, put her head on her arms and cried bitterly.

She was not even sure why she cried. Maybe it was just sheer bitterness, or maybe it was because she had no memories to match those of Marguerite and Alain. Maybe it was this gentle, comfortable house where a man who had not loved her had loved others, strangers to her. Whatever the reason, she wept, heartbroken tears that were almost silent but which tore her apart.

Jenna didn't hear anyone come in. She was too lost in misery, and when she found herself being lifted to her feet embarrassment added itself to the misery. For a second Alain looked down into her drenched eyes and then took her into his arms, holding her fast, well aware that the tears could not be stopped to order.

'It is all right, *petite*,' he said softly, his lips against her hair. 'This is only what I expected.'

'And yet you dragged me into it cruelly,' Jenna sobbed. 'What good will it do you? All this will do is upset your mother.'

'She will not be upset because you will finish your small storm of weeping here and be composed before she sees you,' he ordered, tilting her wet face and looking down at her.

'And what about me? I can be as upset as I like, I suppose?'

'For you, perhaps, it is necessary. A few more walls to tumble.'

He stroked her hair back and cupped her flushed face in his hands. He looked gentle, as if he cared. His glance moved over her face and his thumbs wiped her tears. 'You can weep, Jenna,' he said softly. 'It will help to clear the past. We must make the future happy for you.'

For a moment she stared up at him through glistening eyes, soothed by his hands and the deep sound of his voice. It would be easy simply to drift into the darkness of his eyes, to let everything else slide away. Once again the air was almost alive because he was here. It was something she had never felt before.

He smiled, a look of gathering triumph about him, and Jenna felt a wave of annoyance that stopped any further tears and wrenched her from dreaminess. It was a trick, a way of helping his mother, and a cruel experiment because he thought he knew best.

'You're cruel!' she stormed quietly, blinking at the lingering tears.

'Then stop fighting me as I am sure to win.' He looked at her steadily. 'Before you leave this house you will be cured of all the past.'

'Oh, let me go!' Jenna snapped fretfully. 'I'm tired of being manoeuvred into painful and irritating situations that are supposed to be for my own good. I'm being treated like an incompetent child!'

'Sometimes even big girls cry,' he mused, his lips quirking at her sudden transition from tears to rage. 'Comforting you could become addictive.'

'I've got to help with the meal,' Jenna said uneasily, moving rapidly away from him and searching for her comb. She wanted him out of here fast. He made her feel vulnerable. He had this way of drawing her to him and she always seemed to go. It was dangerous because it left her at his mercy and as far as she knew he had none.

'You will not be welcome in the kitchen,' he warned. 'My mother likes to prepare meals all by herself. Cooking is her hobby and she does not allow well-meaning amateurs. Our task will be to wash the dishes later and I warn you there will be plenty. The debris from her artistic efforts does not interest her in the least.'

'You wash up?' Jenna turned and looked at him in a startled manner. He seemed to her to be too splendid to wash dishes; even Glyn would not think of it, and Alain seemed to her to be a figure of towering importance, the most masculine man she had ever seen.

'Of course I do, with great skill!' He suddenly smiled and pointed to her luggage. 'Get your things sorted out. That way you will not be under her feet. In any case, after dinner you will need an early night. You are here to get well and strong again.'

'I'm here under protest!' Jenna said shortly, noting this return to arrogant organising.

'Tell me that a week from now,' he challenged, and Jenna eyed him firmly.

'I'll be back in England by then.'

'It is a long walk.' Before she could think of a suitable retort he had gone, her door closed quietly behind him.

Jenna wasn't sure who had won, but she rather thought he had. It was surprising that she did not feel embarrassed at being caught in floods of tears. One thing about him that was probably on the plus side: he had the ability to drain away her tension and make her feel better. On the other hand, if he hadn't been so keen on interfering there would not have been any tension because she would not have been here or even in France at all. It really did wipe out all the plus signs.

Dinner was wonderful. Jenna changed into a soft woollen dress of dark blue and tied her hair back in a band. Getting ready helped to restore her calm and, in any case, she felt she owed it to Marguerite to make some effort on this first evening at her house. Jenna could still not think of the place as partly hers. The more she saw of Alain's mother and the more she breathed in the atmosphere of this house, the more she felt outside it all, an intruder who was here to rock the peace of the place, to alter their lives.

She could not understand why Alain had insisted that she be here, unless of course it was to instil in her this very attitude that she was not in any way entitled to a share of their past. After all, he was a very clever man, and sometimes, when he did not think she knew, he gave her some very peculiar looks that made her shivery inside.

She felt the shivers again as she ate her meal and frequently looked up to find him watching her, his eyes on the glitter of her silvery hair.

'Such extravagance,' Marguerite smiled as they ate

dessert—tiny, delicious strawberries in a meringue basket, cream piled on top. 'They are out of season and very expensive, but Alain bought them in Paris this morning, although I imagine it was one of his long-suffering secretaries who was dispatched to buy them.'

Alain merely nodded and smiled and Jenna glanced at him curiously. Glyn had one secretary and he had to share her with Ned Clarke. Alain apparently had several secretaries. Containing her curiosity was impossible.

'You need a lot of secretaries, *monsieur*?' she asked coolly.

'One does the work, the others get under my feet,' he replied sardonically, not helping at all and ignoring her cool formality.

'It is not exactly true,' Marguerite confided as Alain went out to answer the telephone. 'Alain works very hard. He also drives people hard. One secretary could not cope with the work. He is a financier, Jenna, head of Lemarchand-Clement. It is a burden passed on by his father. Nowadays, although the name remains, there is no partner. The whole responsibility rests with Alain and I am pleased to see him here, getting a few days' break, although I imagine that Sunday night will see him speeding back to Paris, whatever we decide to do. He rarely rests. The world of finance is never static.'

Now Jenna knew how he could afford the great house outside Paris. She knew where she had got the notion that he could buy up the whole of her street with the petty cash. He probably could. He could also afford to offer her a great deal of money for her share in this house, enough to tempt anyone. So why had he insisted that she come? Why had he refused to even begin until she was in France?

She was still silently pondering this as he came back into the room and smiled across at his mother.

'Claudine,' he informed her. 'She was all set to arrive

tonight and stay talking, but I told her that we are tired and ready for bed.'

'Well, I am, Alain,' Marguerite said comfortably. 'If you wish to sit up talking with Claudine, however, or walk with her in the moonlight. . .'

'How romantic,' he laughed, sitting back down to drink his coffee. 'There is one flaw in the idea, though. Tonight there is no moon. Also, Jenna must get early nights while she is here.'

'I would not have expected to accompany you on a romantic walk with your girlfriend,' Jenna said hotly, her cheeks flushing at this idea of being relegated to invalidity again. 'I've seen my room and I can make my way to it if you'll draw me a simple map!'

Marguerite began to laugh at this challenge to Alain, and he fixed Jenna with derisive eyes.

'I do not doubt your ability to find your bed. I merely doubt your willingness to go to it. We must get you well.'

'I'll wash the dishes now,' Jenna said, quietly furious. She would not have gone to bed and she knew it. She was intrigued to know what sort of a woman could handle Alain Lemarchand and she had intended to linger and find out.

Marguerite did not protest. She took her coffee into the other room and Alain stayed. He walked across and opened a door in the banked whiteness of the equipment by the wall,

'A dishwasher, *mademoiselle*,' he announced in amusement. 'We will load it together, *n'est-ce pas*? Much of my great skill with dishes comes from this machine. It has never cracked a cup.'

He simply took things out of her hands and left her standing like a fool, and Jenna fumed silently. Oh, to be able to get the better of this man! Her sadness had vanished for now. She was simply filled with exasperation. She began to wipe the tops down with unnecesssary vigour, muttering crossly when water splashed on her dress.

When she looked up he was leaning elegantly against the table, watching her.

'Would you like to walk in the garden before bed?' he asked seriously.

'In the dark?' Jenna glared at him and he looked at her mockingly.

'There are lights around the house, floodlights by the pool at the back. It may calm you down.'

'I'm quite calm, thank you!' Jenna snapped, flushed with annoyance.

'Very well, *ma chère*. Then we will sit by the fire with my mother before bed.'

'Will you kindly stop this?' Jenna fumed. 'I do not need constant supervision. I'm not a doddery old lady!'

'I never for one moment suspected that you were,' he murmured, his eyes suddenly running over her figure. 'If you wish to be left to your own devices then I will leave you.'

He walked out and Jenna was left with the feeling that she had been decidedly ungracious, of uncertain temper and rather childish. His words of a few days ago came unbidden into her mind. 'Scratch me and I bite.' At this rate he might just carry out his threat. She hurried after him to apologise, but when she got to the salon he was not there. Alain had gone to bed, his mother said, and it was not long before they followed, the quiet, comfortable house silent around them.

In her room, Jenna undressed and went to bed, but she lay awake, waiting for grief to hit her. It did not. Her newly acquired temper seemed to have chased grief away for now, or maybe her mind was too shaken up with Alain and his dominance to linger on her father tonight, in spite of being in the house where he had lived.

This of course could not go on and she had no intention of staying. When Alain went back to Paris she would go with him and then fly home. She felt she would have done her duty by Marguerite and even by her father for Marguerite's sake. As to Alain Lemarchand, she owed him no duty at all and certainly no favours. He was probably a terrible boss, she mused sleepily. He would drive everyone to the end of endurance.

Light came flooding into the room, startling her, making her open her eyes again. She was more startled than ever to find that it was the moon, full and bright, riding the night sky like a silver chariot. He had said there was no moon tonight for walking with Claudine. It wasn't true. Maybe he didn't know?

Jenna closed her eyes again and drifted into sleep with a tantalising thought uppermost in her mind. He had offered to walk with her and obviously it would have been in the moonlight, house lights not withstanding. What was he up to? It would all have to be thought out carefully—preferably after she got back to England because she was beginning to think that it would be unwise to put a foot wrong with Alain Lemarchand.

Jenna slept late and arrived downstairs next day feeling guilty and flustered, very glad that Alain was not there to pin her with merciless dark eyes.

'Alain has gone to visit Claudine's parents,' Marguerite informed her as she dished up breakfast. 'That girl is so filled with energy. She was here at seven-thirty and she had walked all the way. In fact I would not be surprised if she had run. Alain has taken her back by car. He will have some difficulty getting away. Claudine has doted on him since she was a child and her parents are pretty much the same.'

'Does she live a long way off?' Jenna asked this more for something to say than anything else. She was not too interested in the vigorous Claudine now that the light of day was here. She was just glad that Alain was out. She seemed to get her good sense back when she couldn't see him.

'The château,' Marguerite said, sitting down to have coffee and keep Jenna company. 'It is about six miles away, impossible to see from here. When we first came here they had just bought it. They were busy restoring it to its past glory. They had a restaurant in Paris and suddenly wished to get out into the country. The château was empty, almost derelict, and they have turned it into a small hotel and restaurant. We must eat there one night. The food is good.'

The idea brought a pang of worry to Jenna. Marguerite was talking as if they would be here for ages. Eat there 'one night', as if there was no real hurry. As far as Jenna was concerned there was every reason to hurry. She wanted to go home. She wanted to get away from France and from Alain. The idea of school was so soothing that she hung on to it tightly.

She had just finished breakfast when Alain drove up to the house and he was alone; Marguerite noted that fact with some surprise.

'Claudine is hardly ever away when Alain is here,' she murmured. 'I had thought she would come back with him as he leaves for Paris on Sunday.'

Jenna was glad that Claudine had not come. She did not want to pretend pleasure at being here and she did not want to witness even more proof of the life that had been led in this house, all of it with her father.

'You feel well today?' Alain walked in, tossing his jacket off. He was in jeans and a white shirt open at the neck, the sleeves rolled up over powerful brown arms, and Jenna experienced an unexpected shiver as she remembered those arms holding her yesterday. The feeling came right out of the blue, startling her, and she didn't answer, much to Alain's amusement. 'Jenna?' He looked down at her and she flushed guiltily.

'Thank you, I feel fine.'

'Very good! Then come with me.' He took her arm, almost lifting her from her seat, leading her out of the kitchen with no further words. Marguerite said nothing. She simply stayed where she was and Jenna found herself being almost propelled outside, too startled to object.

'Where am I going?' Much more speed and her feet would have left the ground. She looked up at Alain in amazement.

'You are going with me,' he announced grimly. 'We should perhaps have started this indoors, but my mother is there. It makes little difference. We will begin from the wrong end and work back.'

She knew instantly what he was talking about. He had not missed the fact that last night she had studiously ignored the paintings in the house. She dug her heels in and stopped.

'I am not going into the barn!'

'*Mon Dieu*, but you are!' Alain kept his punishing grip on her arm and glared down at her. 'Your father was an artist, famous in France, much loved and admired. His daughter will not leave without seeing the work he did!'

'I don't want to! I refuse!'

'You will do as you are told, *mademoiselle*. You will go into the barn and up to his studio. If you continue to behave in this childish manner then I will carry you up there!'

'How *dare* you?' Jenna raged. 'Just who do you think you are?'

'I am Russell's friend, my mother's son and the man who will vanquish the past for you.' He spun her to face him, his eyes once again merciless. 'When you did not come to see him I made myself a vow that you would face reality and not some story that has been hammered into you since childhood. I *knew* Russell Bryant; you did not!'

'I knew all I needed to know,' Jenna reminded him fiercely. 'I was left behind without a qualm.'

He didn't bother to argue further. He glared down

into her determined face and then swept her up in one smooth movement, carrying her into the darkened barn and grimly mounting the wooden steps. She struggled furiously, but it was little use, and at the top of the steps he set her on her feet.

As far as Jenna could see there was nothing there. It was dim with the atmosphere of all old barns—straw, dust, and in this case too the sweet smell of stored apples. There was no sign of a studio and for a minute she expected to find that Alain had been merely frightening her—some hidden cruelty to make her feel uncomfortable, another chance to embarrass her.

He looked down at her, seeing the accusation in her eyes, and his own looks were exasperated.

'I have neither the time nor the inclination to play stupid games,' he snapped. 'Come with me.'

He gripped her wrist firmly and led her to a door. So far she had seen nothing but a normal barn—bales of hay, racks of apples, a few garden tools—but now she found herself forced into the other side of the top floor and it was certainly different, so different in fact that as Alain released her she walked forward of her own volition.

Obviously the top of the long barn had been divided into two. This half was a studio and a good one. It was clear that the light from this side was better even without the addition of huge windows in the roof. It was neat and clean, the smell of paint and thinners taking over from the smell of straw and apples. There was certainly no dust.

There were two easels in the room and on one she saw an unfinished picture. She saw it but she steadfastly refused to look properly. Everything was laid out neatly, brushes and paints on the clean, scrubbed tops. There were paintings stacked at the side of the room—whether finished or not, she did not know—but the thing that was most touching, the thing that stopped her forward momentum was a chair by the lower window, obviously placed to look out over the valley and the distant forest. It was worn and comfortable-looking, like an old, well-loved piece of furniture that had been kept for years. There was a table beside it and a pipe lay on top as if it had been left just for a moment.

She was unprepared for the wave of feeling that hit her; a great empty feeling—loss, grief, bitterness. For the first time she almost seemed to see her father. Remorse and pain clutched at her, almost taking her breath away, and Jenna spun round and took to her heels, taking Alain by surprise so that she was through the door and down the stairs before he caught her.

'Let me go!' As his hand came to her arm she lashed out at him and he caught her close to save himself the trouble of subduing her in any other way.

'I am cruel, *n'est-ce pas*?' he grated, holding her struggling body tightly against his. 'I am mean and vicious, forcing you to face a few ghosts. And there is a ghost there, Jenna, is there not? There is a gentle, much maligned ghost who calls out to you.'

'There's nothing! *You* remember. I don't! I have nothing to remember and I never will have. You can plan as much as you like, but nothing will change facts. The man you knew was a stranger to me and no amount of insisting will alter that.'

Her own pain made her more angry, sharpened her voice, and Alain's attitude hardened.

'So you have no gentleness after all, no imaginations or forgiveness. How painful it must be, *mademoiselle*, to be constantly right.'

'I have a long memory, all of it coloured by the past,' Jenna said bitterly, and he let her go, his expression disgusted.

'You are still a child,' he pointed out scathingly. 'I am wasting my time with you. I have other things to do that are much more important.'

'Then do them and leave me alone!' Jenna burst out.

She knew she was on the edge of tears. Alain did not know what a shock it had been to be dragged up those stairs and to find a room like a small time capsule, the very essence of the man she had not known still lingering there. It made her more sharp, her tongue running away with her. 'Take me to the nearest train. I'll find my own way back to Paris,' she finished angrily.

'Yes. It would please you, would it not?' He turned back to her threateningly. 'You would then be able to assure yourself that all your worst forebodings were correct, that I had brought you here to cheat you out of your share in some shady manner.'

'You can have the house!' Jenna stormed. 'I don't want it. I didn't even want to see it. I'll give my share to your mother and you can tell her you bought it from me; that way she'll be content and you'll be a few pounds better off. I suppose you don't think of much else but making money.'

He looked so thunderous that she would have run had she been able, but the chance did not arise. In one stride he was against her and he caught her to him so savagely that every bit of breath seemed to leave her body.

'You are nothing more than a spoiled, bitter child,' he grated, 'a child with built-in petulance and your mother's way of seeing no other needs but her own.'

'You didn't know my mother. . .'

'I knew your father and none of this was in him. Where else could it have come but from your beautiful, selfish mother? It is too late to help you. She has turned you into an image of herself. Thank God that Russell did not see you.'

His words hit her like small, sharp knives and Jenna raised her hands to claw at him, hurting inside and wanting to hurt back. Her fingers never reached his dark, arrogant and angry face. With a growl of fury he tightened his hold on her and, when she looked up at him with wildly angry eyes, he bent his head and crushed her lips with his own.

Jenna's hands came to his chest in panic—a feeble attempt to push him away, to escape the contact with his mouth—but it was a useless exercise. It was like contact with rock—immovable—the lean, hard body superbly fit and not about to give way before female struggles. His whole attitude was a furious desire to discipline her, and Jenna moaned as her lips were crushed.

It was only when he felt her going limp against him that he stopped and lifted his head. Her lips were swollen against her pale face and the sight of her distress seemed to infuriate him more. There was an ominous tightness to his mouth, a line of white fury, a threat in the dark eyes that burned down at her.

'You make a savage of me, a monster,' he rasped, his breathing tight and heavy. 'I have never felt about any woman as I feel about you. You are an impossible, constant irritation. You are quite right, *mademoiselle*. You will never fit in here. I doubt if there is any place where you could belong comfortably, except perhaps the sterile life you have built for yourself in England. Your instincts tell you to hurry back to it and clearly you are right!'

He let her go abruptly, walking out of the barn, and Jenna sat down on the bottom step of the dusty wooden stairs. She was shaking like a leaf in a storm, bewildered and utterly drained of emotion. She put her hand tentatively to her face, a small, fretful, cry escaping from her bruised lips. He had condemned her and the warmth she had sensed in him from their first meeting had all gone. He was quite prepared to crush her in his desire to force her into seeing what she did not wish to see.

His car swept past the entrance to the barn. He had not gone into the house at all and now he was furiously driving off. She could understand why. In this rage he would only upset his mother, and Jenna put her hands against her hot face. She couldn't go back into the house either. One look at her and Marguerite would know what had happened.

She got unsteadily to her feet and peered outside. It was all right for Alain; he had simply got into his car and driven away. Jenna had nowhere to run, no hiding-place to escape to until she recovered. If she went anywhere it would have to be on her own two feet. She looked cautiously around and then walked away from the house, making for the road that had led here, the long, twisting road from the main highway.

CHAPTER SIX

IT TOOK a very short time indeed, and with every step Jenna's trembling lessened, although she refused to think about the last few moments in the barn with Alain. She heard a noise, but, before she could take any evasive action, a cycle came spinning round the corner and the sharp eyes of the girl who had been cleaning the farm were on her intently.

Jenna's face flushed with embarrassment at the way the girl watched in amused surprise. There was a look about her that said everything, and Jenna didn't need it spelt out. She looked as if she had been kissed thoroughly—her fair hair was tangled, her lips full and red, and even her own blushing made the point clearer.

'*Bonjour*, *mademoiselle*.'

To Jenna's annoyance the girl slid from her cycle and walked it forward.

'Good morning.' Jenna felt more able to cope with dignity in her own language and the girl's face creased into a knowing smile.

'Ah! You are the English guest that *madame* has at the farm, *n'est-ce pas*? I saw you yesterday and Mademoiselle Rabier knows about you. You will easily become lost here, *mademoiselle*. If you are looking for Monsieur Alain, I passed him on the main road. He is probably going to the château. Most of his time here is spent with Mademoiselle Rabier.'

For some reason she was determined to drive the fact home, and Jenna felt rising anger to add to her other feelings. The girl was studying her as if she was an amusing spectacle and Jenna assumed that she was. *Monsieur* was on his way to see his lady-love and *she* was alone, but she had been in somebody's arms. As there were no other masculine arms but Alain's then that too was obvious and the girl's knowing and amused looks explained it all thoroughly.

'I am well aware that Monsieur Alain is at the château,' she snapped. 'I'm going for a walk. Goodbye!'

'You will be lost, *mademoiselle*.' The girl mounted her cycle and imparted this gloomy information with a cheerfulness that stated her wish to see Jenna disappear altogether. An ally of Claudine, no doubt! As far as Jenna was concerned they could all band together and explode. This was another humiliation that Alain had forced on her.

If he came back he would see her walking away from the house, walking down the track as if she were on her way back to Paris. He would certainly conclude that she was up to some adolescent mischief and take her to task again. She couldn't face that. At the moment she felt she would attempt to kill him. A path into the woods appeared on her right-hand side and she stepped on to it gladly. A few more steps and the trees hid her.

It was cool, a slight breeze drifting over her face, calming the heat of her skin. The face that had paled with fright and shock had now flushed. Her swollen lips burned and she knew she must look a mess. No wonder the girl had stared at her and drawn her own conclusions. It would be a few hours before she could face Marguerite, and no doubt the girl, Marie, would be very quick to tell Alain's mother that she had seen the Englishwoman wandering into the woods like a lunatic.

At the back of her mind, Jenna knew it would be all too easy to become lost. At some stage this wood became forest and no small forest either. At the moment she was completely orientated. She knew where the track was and she also knew where the main road joined it. She turned in that direction even though it meant leaving the path. When she had the sound of the sparse traffic in her ears she would sit down and rest, then she would walk back by the track.

The turmoil inside her had not by any means subsided and she put her hand to her lips, testing the surface carefully. His action had been almost instant and she knew he had wanted to beat her instead. It was only because he was a civilised man that he had not. Jenna grimaced at the thought. Civilised? How civilised had he been, after all? The kiss had been cynical, insolent. It had also been her first real brush with masculine anger and the effect frightened her. It was easy enough to rationalise, to calmly explain to herself why he had done that, but her senses went their own way, remembering not the insult but the strength of his arms, the tang of his skin, the instinctive feeling that his lips had wanted to soften and soothe her.

What nonsense! He had been angry and nothing more. One thing was sure: when she met him again it would be Alain who would feel uncomfortable because there was no forgiving an action like that. Jenna came back to the present rapidly and painfully as she tripped over a fallen and partially sunken log. For the past few minutes she had not really been paying much attention to the direction and she looked round worriedly. Now she was not orientated at all and for all she knew she could have been going round in circles.

It was a great relief therefore to hear the sound of a passing car, its speed assuring her that the main road was in front of her. All she had to do was go forward and then turn to her left as she found the road. Her arm was stinging and as she looked down she was surprised to see that she had also grazed the skin there. She must look quite a sight. The sooner she got back on to the track the better. If she met the girl Marie on the way back there would be even more for her to tell Mademoiselle Rabier!

The road suddenly appeared through the thinning trees and Jenna had to scramble down a bank, cross a ditch and she was standing on the firm tarmac of the main highway. She sincerely hoped that she could make it to the track before any car came because she knew exactly what a mess she looked. She had looked unkempt enough to amuse Marie earlier; now, she looked even worse. Dragged through a hedge backwards was probably exactly how she looked. She was grazed and grass-stained from her fall, even more dishevelled because of having to fight her way through massed bushes. When she put her hand to her hair she felt small twigs and she was hastily removing them when a car slid to a halt beside her.

'*Tout va bien, mademoiselle*? *Est-ce que je peux vous aider*?'

Jenna looked up from her gloomy contemplation of her appearance to find a young man watching her from a racy-looking open-topped car. She had to admit that he looked more worried about her than threatening and this brought a small smile of relief to her face.

'I—I'm sorry. I. . .'

'Ah! You are English? I heard at the château that there was an English girl staying close by. I heard the daily cleaner saying——'

'Marie?' Jenna asked with a rueful look.

'The very one.' He looked at her odd appearance and then frowned. 'You have had an accident, *mademoiselle*?'

'Not really,' Jenna confessed with an embarrassed look. 'I went for a walk in the woods and got lost. I also fell a few times.'

'I will take you back to the farm.' He was out of the car very speedily and Jenna felt a quick burst of fright. Just becasue he knew about her it did not mean he was at all reliable.

'I can walk,' she managed hastily.

'But why should you? I will have you back in no time at all.' He took her arm firmly and Jenna was in quite a dilemma. To struggle would seem like madness and she already felt less than cool as it was. He might very well be staying at the château, but that didn't mean anything. She had stupidly given him the name Marie and he had latched on to it.

No decision was necessary as it turned out. They were still standing right there as another car drew up behind them with a scream of tyres and Alain emerged, tall, dark and definitely forbidding.

'*Qu'est-ce qui se passe ici*?'

His sharp question brought a flush to the face of the man who was so insistent upon helping Jenna, and she decided to get her word in first in view of Alain's forbidding looks.

'I'm being offered a lift back to the farm, that's all.' It was difficult to look haughty and defiant when she knew exactly what a mess she looked and still held the memory of why she had got into this state. Even so, now that Alain was there she felt safe enough to go with the man anyhow. Alain looked as if he would follow an inch behind them all the way to the farm.

'How kind,' Alain murmured scathingly. 'Fortunately I am here and therefore I can save you a trip, Bernard.'

Jenna was a bit surprised that Alain knew this man and the fact that he knew him wasn't making him any more gracious, either. However, the man gave ground and that didn't surprise her at all. Alain was glaring at both of them, not one ounce of give in his attitude.

'Very good. If you are sure?' Bernard smiled at Jenna and looked even then as if her wanted her to refuse to go with Alain. There was no decision to make this time either.

'*I* am sure!' Alain said sharply, and Jenna found another hand on her arm, just as firm and decidedly more forceful. She wondered rather wildly for a moment if they would both refuse to let go and imagined herself the unwilling participant in an unlikely tug of war, but Bernard took one look at Alain and released her.

'I will see you again, *mademoiselle*,' he murmured, but Alain was already putting Jenna into his car.

'It will be difficult,' he said pithily. 'She lives in the north of England.'

'Er—thank you,' Jenna managed breathlessly, smiling at Bernard from the safety of Alain's car. They swept away before she could get any reply, and she wasn't too sure of safety, either—Alain looked murderous.

'Are you completely devoid of any kind of common sense?' he rasped as they roared off down the road. 'Is it your habit to accept lifts from any stranger who happens upon you?'

'I wasn't going to,' Jenna protested. 'At least, I hadn't made my mind up.'

'What mind?' he grated rudely, going on before she could answer. 'In any case, it is clear that he had made his mind up. You were about to be hauled into his car, whatever your mind decided.'

'If he's so untrustworthy then how is it that you know him?' she asked with shaky triumph.

'I do not know him,' he snapped. 'I have been introduced and I was not impressed. Bernard Villette is a friend of Claudine and staying at the château.'

Ah! That explained it. Bernard Villette was a rival for Claudine's affections. Jenna was surprised how gloomy that made her feel. Alain had rescued her as if he cared what became of her, and she supposed he had to, anyway; she was, as he had said, his responsibility. All the same, his anger had been tempered with thoughts of Claudine with Bernard, and Jenna sat silently, moodily contemplating the trees until they turned into the track to the house. She had gone much further than she had imagined. It would have been a long walk to here, and no doubt some other person would have been offering a dubious lift by the time she arrived.

'Why are you in this state?' Alain suddenly snapped at her.

'I went for a walk in the woods. I—I went further than I intended and I fell over. That's why I. . .'

He stopped the car and turned to look down at her, his eyes running over her, seeing the state she was in, the grazed leg and arm, her rather dirty hands.

'A few days ago you were quite ill,' he pointed out grimly. 'Now you are setting off on mad expeditions.' His eyes raced over her hair and face and his expression suddenly softened. 'Why did you go off into the woods? You knew it was foolish.'

'Well, I couldn't very well just go inside, could I?' Jenna asked miserably, avoiding his eyes. 'It was all right for you. you just got into the car and roared away. I—I couldn't just go in and—and I had nowhere to go so. . .'

'*Pauvre petite*. I am treating you very badly, am I not?' His hand curved around her face, tilting it up, and Jenna had no option but to meet his dark eyes.

'Your mother would have noticed. . .'

'And realised that her son is a villain,' he finished for her. 'I am not always a villain,' he added quietly. His thumb was probing the hollow of her cheek and Jenna flushed uncomfortably.

'I know that,' she assured him breathlessly. She couldn't understand this eagerness to forgive him, but it was definitely there. 'I know it's just me. I can't change my way of thinking, though, and I want to go home, even if you think it's childish.'

'I do not think it childish. I think it ill-advised. I also know it is a desire driven by fear. You are afraid of what I will force you to see. I understand too, Jenna.'

'Then can't you just give in gracefully and save us all a lot of trouble?' Jenna asked a bit desperately. It brought a smile to the dark face.

'I am not a villain, but I make no claims to being graceful,' he murmured. 'However, we can at least repair the damage I have done.' His eyes were on her lips and Jenna looked at him with wide, worried eyes.

'There's no real damage,' she said quickly. 'I know I shouted and was unfair. If you can just get me into the house without your mother seeing. . .'

'It is most unlikely.' He smiled down at her. 'We can only hope to fool her by being friends.'

His head bent towards her and once again Jenna lifted her hands to ward him off in a panic-stricken way, but her fingers felt useless. They seemed to be paralysed as they encountered the hard wall of his chest, and his lips covered hers and met no resistance at all. He kissed her lingeringly as if he had all the time in the world and she felt a shudder run through her at the response he was forcing from her with so little effort. His mouth was moving warm and hard over hers but this time with no intention of punishing, and Jenna had a wild urge to move closer and feel his arms tighten. He was making her need this and alarm bells rang wildly, but she ignored them.

'It would be so easy to be friends with you, *petite*,' he murmured against her ear. 'Don't run away from me. I want you here.'

She was utterly pliant as his lips traced her neck and cheeks, and when they brushed her own again she felt warmth flood over her. His lips hardened and he lifted her closer, cupping her head and kissing her deeply when she made no move to get away. She knew what the singing in the air had been and her arms crept around his neck as he drew her closer still.

Alain lifted his head and looked down at her and she was still staring mesmerised into his dark eyes when a voice she knew already spoke almost in her ear.

'*Au revoir*, *monsieur*, *mademoiselle*.' It was Marie on her way home, her cycle slowed down as she took in the interesting spectacle, and Jenna looked up, startled, catching the gleam in the girl's eyes. Jenna's face flooded with colour and Alain slowly let her go, leaning forward to start the car. She knew then why he had done it, why he had kissed her and taken his time. He was well aware of how long Marie stayed here and he could calculate just exactly when she would be passing. If Claudine had a friend staying at the château then Alain was showing that he also had a willing friend.

'I suppose you think that was funny?' Jenna spat out angrily, her face burning with humiliation.

'I was not feeling particularly amused,' he said sardonically. 'You found it humorous?'

'I did not! I found it despicable. If you imagine you can use me to remind Mademoiselle Rabier of what she's missing by paying attention to her friend Bernard then you can think again!'

'She was not here, *petite*.'

'Her spy was! And you can stop this "*petite*" business!'

'Very well, *mademoiselle*. We will return to formality.' He simply set off with no further glance at her, and Jenna seethed. He had rendered her almost mindless there and it had all been a cheap trick, not even part of his wish to get her to accept her father. It had been a sideline to use her to further his love-life.

'Extremely formal, if you please,' she said with stiff anger. 'I will also return to England, and any further attempt to keep me here I shall count as kidnapping.'

'Since that will no doubt bring your cold-blooded legal friend down upon us, I agree,' he said derisively. 'But you are wasting your talents with him, *mademoiselle*, and will live to regret it. He does not have any scope for passion, it seems, and yet you are sweetly soft to hold, wonderfully submissive to kiss. You are as delicious as you look. I doubt if he could match your potential.'

'He's a gentleman!' Jenna hissed.

'He is an imbecile,' Alain corrected drily. He pulled up at the farm and got out to open the door for her before she could move. There was no way she would be able to avoid Marguerite, and Jenna's anger faded a little at the prospect of facing Alain's mother looking as she did.

'Your mother will know,' Jenna said anxiously.

'So?' He looked down at her sardonically, his long lips twisted in a caustic smile. 'She is discreet and she is French. She will assume that her villainous son has been involved in yet more villainy.' He walked off in front of her and Jenna had no choice at all; she followed and only had time to glare at him reproachfully as he opened the door and stood aside for her, and then Marguerite was there.

'Jenna!' Her smile of welcome faded as she took in the sorry state of Jenna's appearance. 'What happened?'

Alain said nothing at all and Jenna had to think fast, keeping as much to the truth as possible. She was not cut out for subterfuge.

'Rather stupidly, I went for a walk in the woods and I got lost. I—er—managed to get to the road and—and Alain rescued me.'

'Oh, Jenna,' Marguerite exclaimed in horror. 'I was happily thinking that you were out with Alain and quite safe. Please don't wander off again.'

'No. I certainly won't,' Jenna promised. Safe with Alain? That was really funny and he looked suspiciously close to laughter. But then why not? He had won hands down—again. Jenna smiled rather wanly and went to take a shower. No, she would not wander off again, she would go post-haste to England and Alain could get on with his intrigues and his high-powered business. He must be very tricky to deal with, she thought darkly. He was ruthless, and as to being a villain—he probably was.

Jenna took her time. She was more scratched than she had realised and it felt as if every small insect in the wood had landed in her hair. The shower was wonderfully soothing and afterwards she spent a long time drying her hair and putting on her make-up. With Alain around she felt she needed as much camouflage as possible. She put on white trousers and a long, sage-green tunic top.

Whatever she felt inside, she was certainly going to look cool and composed outside. Now she could face them.

When she got downstairs they were both waiting for her, so obviously waiting that she stopped dead and looked alarmed. Now what?

'We are going out to lunch,' Alain informed her, reading her expression with little difficulty. 'I booked lunch at the château and it is time we were off.'

'I'm sorry I took so long——' Jenna started apologetically, but he interrupted smoothly, standing and motioning them both to the door.

'No matter. It was worth waiting for. Cool and beautiful, *n'est-ce pas, Maman*?'

'Very beautiful,' Marguerite said softly. She looked sad and Jenna couldn't understand it at all. As to cool, she was no such thing. She was now in a state every time she looked at Alain. It was like waiting for a bomb to explode, because she never knew what he would do next. Who would have thought when she had first seen him in England that he would drag her into his life, order her about, kiss her? Her cheeks flooded with colour and he slanted a derisive look at her as he opened the car door.

'We are not taking you to an uncivilised place, Jenna,' he murmured. 'Panic will not be necessary. In any case, I will be there to rescue you should the need arise.'

She made a move to pass him and join Marguerite, who had established herself in the back seat, but his arm barred her way.

'The front,' he ordered quietly. 'That way you can get a good look at the château as we approach and also I can have the pleasure of your company.'

'It won't be pleasant,' Jenna muttered, embarrassed by this conspiracy.

'I cannot see why not. Not too long ago your company was most pleasant for a while.'

It being impossible to hit him with Marguerite looking on, Jenna slid into the passenger seat and kept silent.

Once again she was being used to wave in front of Claudine and she knew it. She regretted the effort she had put into her appearance. Almost everything she did played right into Alain's hands.

The château was, as she had been told, not too far away. It was so well hidden by forest, however, that they were almost upon it before she really had the chance to look. Her first thoughts were that it was a great shame to turn such a wonderful building into a restaurant and hotel. It seemed utterly incongruous that there were cars parked outside on the wide circular drive—carriages would have looked more appropriate.

The place was not a very grand huge château, but it was imposing and romantic nevertheless, with lawned terraces sweeping down to the drive, great old trees around it and a small lake to one side that actually lapped the lower walls. As they stopped Jenna was very reluctant to get out. Suddenly, she didn't want to meet Claudine Rabier. She had the feeling that this morning's events would have been faithfully reported by Marie and she sincerely hoped that the girl did not add to her earnings by serving as a waitress here.

It was impossible to refuse to move, though, and Jenna found herself being urged out of the car and across the gravelled drive towards the ivy-covered entrance of the château. Marguerite was busily describing the place to her and pointing out how well it had been restored, but Jenna was more aware of Alain's dark silence. She hung on to one thought determinedly. Tomorrow was Sunday. As far as she knew, Alain was going back to Paris in the afternoon and *she* was going with him, whether he liked it or not!

At least the Rabiers had had the good sense to leave the inside of the château as it had been, at any rate on this floor. The only alteration that had been made was the lighting, and Jenna was not at all sure that she approved. The family seemed to have a bias towards pink. The wall lights in the great stone walls were bedecked with pink silk shades. The cloths on the small round tables were pink in another shade. The flowers, she noted, were not real, and, glancing at Marguerite, she was amused to note that the dark, finely arched brows were arched even further with faint disapproval.

It was cool and dark, the stone floor scattered with rugs, and it was not long before Jenna decided it was too cool and too dark. The latter problem was taken care of as a waiter came to show them to their table; he lit a pink candle and Jenna suddenly felt amused, her nervous state leaving her. She shot a look at Alain, but looked away very speedily when she found his eyes on the sudden curve of her lips.

'The food is good,' he murmured sardonically, 'and normally the company is excellent.'

He was always quick to appreciate her thoughts, Jenna noted uneasily, and the excellent company soon came threading through the tables to join them. She didn't need to be told that this was Claudine because the newcomer swept up to Alain and bent to kiss his cheek with an air of one who was quite accustomed to his undivided attention.

'*Chéri*! I was beginning to think I would not see you today. Brigitte is having a party and when I knew you were here I naturally said we would go.'

'What is natural about it?' Alain looked at her with a great deal of indulgence, but Jenna was busily reorganising her thoughts. So he hadn't been here this morning while she was forcing her way through the woods? She had assumed that he had come to Claudine as soon as he had finished chastising her, but clearly he hadn't.

'You always spend your time with me when you are here. Does he not, Marguerite?' This appeal to Alain's mother had Marguerite smiling with similar indulgence.

'He seems to do,' she agreed. 'It is only what I expect.'

'Well, there you are!' Claudine pouted. 'Say you'll come, Alain?'

'It is not at all easy,' Alain pointed out with the same teasing that was beginning to set Jenna's teeth on edge. 'We now have a guest, as you can see. Jenna, allow me to introduce Claudine Rabier.'

'Yes. I had heard that you were staying at the farm,' Claudine stated, condescending to look at Jenna for the first time. 'You're not a bit like your father. He wasn't fair like you.'

Jenna's face froze. Here was another person who knew her father better than she did, a person who was pointing it out with little subtlety.

'My mother was fair,' she said briefly.

'And beautiful,' Alain added unexpectedly. 'Jenna takes after her mother.' Claudine didn't seem to know that this was a cruel dig at Jenna; she only appeared to note the word 'beautiful', and with that her interest faded, her eyes going back to Alain.

She was certainly vigorous-looking, Jenna thought. It would not be at all difficult to imagine this person running from here to the farm and back again without pause for breath. She was smaller than Jenna with none of Jenna's slender, willowy height, but she was so healthy-looking that the fact in itself gave her an added attraction. She was pretty and crisply dark, her hair short and curling round a pointed face. At the moment her eyes were coaxing as they turned on Alain, but when she had looked at Jenna there had been a coldness that was quickly hidden. She did not encourage competition and her expression made that plain.

'Shall we go to the party?' she wheedled, and Alain sat back with a smile.

'If you like. We will take Jenna and my mother too.'

'Oh, no, thank you!' Marguerite laughed. 'I have no desire to attend parties. Jenna will enjoy it, though.'

'It's kind of you,' Jenna put in quickly. 'However, I intend to stay with Marguerite. Enjoy yourselves.'

It was the first time she had called his mother by her name, and Alain looked at her intently. Marguerite's face flushed with pleasure and Claudine looked from one to the other very suspiciously.

'Very well,' Alain said slowly. 'I will take you, Claudine.'

'Oh, *chéri*! I knew you would,' she gurgled. 'I even have my dress all ready and laid out on the bed.'

She almost danced away and Alain murmured sardonically, 'Now perhaps we can eat?' He signalled the waiter over and Marguerite leaned across to Jenna.

'You do not have to stay in to be with me, Jenna, dear,' she said softly.

'I prefer your company,' Jenna stated with no attempt at subterfuge, and Marguerite burst into laughter.

'Alain! What have you been saying to Jenna? You may have to change your attitude because I really think she is quite annoyed with you.'

'She does not take orders too well,' Alain growled with a sidelong glance at Jenna's mutinous face. 'Even orders for her own safety are disregarded. It is as well that she has chosen to stay with you this evening because there is no way I will leave you alone at the farm.'

'I'll be all right, Alain,' Marguerite said quickly, but he frowned and shook his head.

'We are not about to put that to the test. The place is isolated. If you intend to live there finally then there must be some sort of companion or housekeeper.'

'Well, Jenna and I will be all right together,' Marguerite said firmly.

'For tonight,' he agreed. 'When I leave tomorrow, however, I will not permit you to stay. Jenna is determined to go home. You will both return to Paris with me.'

That took care of her escape plans, Jenna mused

thankfully. It also put an end to any enjoyment of the meal, because Marguerite seemed to sink into a gloomy silence that worried Jenna far more than it did Alain. He could at least have waited until tomorrow to lay down the law so firmly. She shot him an angry look, but all she received in return was a derisively raised eyebrow, and, when Claudine came back to their table and pulled up a chair with the ease of a spoiled favourite, Alain gave her all his attention and left Jenna to try to pull Marguerite back into some sort of pleasure at this irritating treat.

'Did you enjoy it?' Alain asked quietly as they slowly made their way to the car later. He had not easily shaken Claudine off—not that he had tried—and his arm around the girl's waist had irritated Jenna unbelievably. Now though, they were alone, walking to the car, Marguerite having been waylaid by an acquaintance.

'Not particularly,' Jenna said ungraciously. 'The place was dark and too cold and I'm afraid I prefer Marguerite's cooking.' She knew she was deliberately goading him to anger and even as she did it she was annoyed with herself. Why couldn't she just leave things and be coolly polite? There was only tomorrow morning and then he would be out of her life. The trouble was that he got under her skin.

'You are behaving like a spoiled child again.' Instead of being angry he laughed. 'What is wrong, *petite*? You do not like Claudine?'

'I've no thoughts on that subject,' Jenna said fiercely. 'As I shall not be seeing her again it would be pointless. She's your problem.'

'She is no problem,' he murmured smoothly. 'She has been falling at my feet since she was a child.'

'An astonishing lack of discernment,' Jenna pointed out waspishly, not looking at him. 'Maybe she'll grow out of it?'

'I think it is too late,' he assured her in amusement. 'She is already two years older than you.'

'Don't despair. As you pointed out, I'm childish.'

'Only in your actions,' he corrected with silky malice, 'not in your reactions.'

Jenna stopped and faced him angrily, but before she could speak he tilted her face with a strong brown hand.

'I also pointed out that if you scratch me I bite,' he reminded her softly. 'You have not yet escaped, Jenna. You are still in France.'

'Let me tell you——!' Jenna began heatedly, but he glanced away as his mother came towards them across the lawn.

'Not now, *ma chère*,' he warned. 'My mother is almost here and she would be startled if I had to kiss you into silence. Claudine would probably collapse.'

'And of course you imagine I would stay still and do nothing?' Jenna raged, her face flushed and embarrassed.

'Probably,' he murmured ironically. 'After all, that is what you did last time.'

CHAPTER SEVEN

LATER, Jenna waited anxiously for Alain to go out. She realised that she was much too aware of him, but this should have come as no surprise. She had been too aware of him since their first meeting and he knew it. He was right when he had said that they had a peculiar reaction to each other. The feeling was growing each time they met, and Alain's dark eyes told her he knew.

When at last he went out as the dusk was gathering she was very glad to see him go. At least she could breathe properly when he was out of the house. As his car went away she gave a great sigh of relief and Marguerite shot her an amused glance.

'He is too powerful, *n'est-ce pas*? With Alain it is all or nothing. I suppose you have found that out already. He is like his father, but, as I said before, he is kind.'

Jenna had doubts about that now, but she let it go. All the same, she was intrigued. She wanted to know more about Alain and he had told her nothing at all. She was pleased when Marguerite invited her to help with the evening meal. In view of Alain's remarks on the subject she felt quite honoured, even though she was only given small tasks. It gave her the chance to be with Marguerite, though, and they talked quite easily as they moved around the kitchen.

'What was Alain's father like?' she asked at last when her desire to know about Alain overcame her shyness.

'To look at? Like Alain in many ways, but his hardness showed through. He did not have Alain's humour or compassion. He was business all the way with little time for us. Mostly I was ignored, although I had every material thing I could wish for. Alain became interesting to his father when he showed that he was exceptionally clever and had the same flair for finance. After that I very much doubt if Alain could have taken another path but into the firm. Even before university he was being schooled to take over one day. Luckily he was interested, but there was no gentleness in our lives until. . .until. . .'

'Until you met my father,' Jenna finished for her softly.

'I did not mean to speak about this,' Marguerite assured her worriedly, but Jenna smiled and got on with her task.

'It doesn't matter. None of it was your fault.'

'Nor Russell's, Jenna. I beg you to understand that. We did not have a wild and romantic love-affair. Your mother divorced him and we had many interests in common.' She stopped and bit her lip anxiously. 'We will stop talking about it.'

'It's all right,' Jenna said quietly. 'Perhaps I would have liked him too—if I'd known him.'

'Jenna. . .!' Whatever Marguerite had been about to say she did not continue and later changed the subject with firmness that told Jenna she would not bring it up again. There was a thread of affection growing between them and she knew that as well as Jenna did. Apparently she was not prepared to risk this for the sake of pleading Russell's cause.

Jenna was glad. The ghosts were very close to the surface here in the Dordogne, here in this house, and Jenna was torn in many ways. There was the memory of past hurt—great hurt and anger. There was also this feeling that any attempt to search into her father's past would be disloyal to her mother. Things were best left alone. There was also Alain, who filled her thoughts for most of the time.

After dinner they talked about lots of things, each carefully skirting the thing uppermost in their minds. Marguerite told Jenna that perhaps finally Alain would marry Claudine; at any rate, she added with amusement, he would if it was left to Claudine. Jenna found that she didn't want to know, in fact she didn't want to know to an almost frantic extent. One more night here and they would all go back to Paris and she would go home to England. It would be the end of her time being in any way close to Alain.

When Marguerite went to bed, Jenna went too, but sleep was far from her. It had been a day of many upsets. Twice Alain had kissed her. She had faced a certain amount of humiliation again at the hands of that wretched Marie, but the thing that stayed in her mind was the feel of Alain's arms and the tang of his skin. It was quite ridiculous and so very obvious that he was doing this for many dubious reasons of his own.

He was not a man to give way easily and he had clearly set his heart on making her recognise her father. It was all for Marguerite's sake. Except for the little meanness about Claudine, his nasty trick of kissing her when he knew that Marie would see them. Everything he had done that had seemed at all kind had been part of a plan to make her face her past for his mother's sake. No doubt it would give Marguerite some comfort to be able to be warm and friendly with Russell's daughter, but it was too big a price to pay. Jenna knew it.

She got up and put on her dressing-gown. Marguerite was sleeping and Jenna crept downstairs in the silent house and made her way to the kitchen to fix herself a milky drink. Her father seemed to be all around her in this house. Not as much as he had been in the studio, but he was here all the same. She kept remembering that he had walked in this room, sat in the chairs, eaten at the table. She took her drink to the salon, where the remains of the fire still glowed, and after a while she put on the lamps and went slowly across to look at the paintings.

Somehow she knew which ones he had done, even before she saw the signature. They were impressionist paintings, glowing colours that swirled into form. There were some of the Dordogne, one of this house he had loved. Another was of the château, the water of the lake glistening in the evening sun. Unexpectedly there was a portrait, and she knew it was good although her knowledge of art was skimpy to say the least. It was Marguerite as she had been many years ago, and Jenna saw what her father had seen, what she herself saw now—the attraction of kindness, of calm good humour. He had painted his best friend and his wife and Jenna couldn't fault it.

She was so wrapped up in the portrait that she heard nothing until the clink of glass told her she was not alone, and as she spun round she found Alain turning from pouring himself a drink. He said nothing. After one all-encompassing look at her he simply sat down with his brandy and stared into the dying fire.

'You're back early.' Obviously he was not going to speak and Jenna was embarrassed at being caught here, more embarrassed still at the idea of walking haughtily to her room without a word.

'I do not like discos and noisy youth,' he said abruptly, continuing to stare into the fire.

'I—I suppose Claudine was disappointed after getting ready to go,' Jenna stammered. She hated herself for wanting to know, but the words just seemed to leap out. He simply shrugged unconcernedly.

'I took her there. I also stayed for the required time that politeness dictates. No doubt Bernard Villette will bring her back.'

It explained his mood. He was angry that Bernard had gone too. Claudine had probably dropped that on him at the last minute. Well, it was nothing to do with her.

'I'll go to bed now. Goodnight,' she said quickly. She had been kneeling in an easy-chair to look at the painting at that side of the room and as she moved he suddenly looked across at her intently, his face moody.

'So you looked at his work?'

'I couldn't sleep. I—I was just wandering around with my drink.' She indicated the glass of milk on the table and moved to pick it up and take it into the kitchen. He was on his feet so swiftly that she drew back automatically, worried about being here at night in her dressing-gown, and her action brought a black frown to his face.

'I am not about to attack you,' he rasped. 'If you feel somewhat vulnerable in your dressing-gown let me remind you I have seen you in your nightdress and not felt driven to mindless passion.'

'I didn't. . . You—you made me jump. . .' It was clearly not a time for any angry rejoinder and she almost fled to the kitchen, her heart beating like a hammer. He made her feel strange—he always had done—and now, when he was so angry, she was almost afraid. She was just getting her breath back when the kitchen door opened and he was there, glaring at her.

'You intend to hide here all night? You are scared to pass me on the way to the stairs?' he grated. 'Hide under the table, *mademoiselle*, and when I am in my room I will bang on the floor and the coast will be clear.'

'I'm not hiding,' Jenna said firmly, making herself meet the dark, angry eyes. 'I was just wondering whether to have some more milk, that's all,' she lied, 'and I'm not scared either.'

'You are,' he snapped. 'I am not always a monster who will attack you.'

'Then maybe you should get control of your temper and go to bed,' Jenna said as coolly as she could manage. 'Don't imagine you can take it out on me because things have not gone right for you at the party. If you're jealous of Bernard then you should get engaged and he'll know that Claudine is spoken for.'

He turned away in disgust, his hand on the kitchen door.

'You are idiotic! Another trait from your mother, no doubt.'

'Will you stop making snide remarks about my mother?' Jenna raised her voice, anger sweeping away her slight fear and her other unmanageable feelings. In her annoyance she grabbed his arm and he spun round with frightening speed, his dark eyes leaping at her.

'Did I not tell you that I bite?' he asked menacingly. It had her dropping her aggressive stance immediately, and as he advanced she retreated until she felt the table hard and unyielding against her back. Her quick change from aggression to alarm amused him apparently, because his hard mouth twisted in derision.

'Now what, *mademoiselle*?' he asked softly. 'Do you scratch my face, scream for my mother or force your way past me to run?'

'I'm simply going to bed,' Jenna said breathlessly, facing him with anxiety. 'Don't touch me!' she added in a panic-stricken voice as his arms suddenly came around her.

'Why not?' he derided, pulling her away from the table and against the hard warmth of his body. 'I have had a very boring evening, a very frustrating evening, and at least you are beautiful.'

'Please! Don't!' She gasped out the words as his dark head bent towards her, but instead of kissing her lips he let his mouth trail over her neck, nuzzling under her hair until shivers started to race down her spine. She knew she had to fight free now and she tried, but his grip on her merely tightened.

'Stop fighting me.' His voice was slurred and she wondered just how many brandies he had had tonight to cure him of his frustration.

'Let me go, Alain,' she ordered as firmly as her trembling would allow, but he was not at all impressed.

'I will let you go when I do not feel so frustrated,' he murmured thickly. 'I am not going to hurt you, *chérie*.' He looked down at her, his smile darkly menacing. 'At least, I am not going to hurt you very much.'

Before she could make another move, his mouth covered hers and he gathered her so tightly to him that making any move was impossible. He was ruthless, holding her so close that she could hardly breathe, and his kiss was devastating. As he plundered her mouth Jenna was faintly aware that there was very little anger left in him; this was complete sensuality, no doubt because he had been robbed of an evening with Claudine in his arms.

Jenna murmured anxiously and his hand slid to her throat as he pulled her to his shoulder. She could feel his fingers moving over the slenderness of her neck like gentle questions, gauging her reaction, lingering against the racing pulse, assessing her feelings. What he discovered pleased him because his lips softened against hers and his questing hand slid beneath her hair to find her tender nape and soothe wonderfully.

If he had moved his mouth from hers she would have come to her senses, resisted, but he did no such thing. His tongue teased at her lips until she opened them helplessly, allowing him to deepen the kiss, his tongue stroking hers in an act of burning sexuality that had her sagging against him.

He felt the surrender and his hand moved back to her throat, his long fingers exploring again before plunging down to invade the neck of her dressing-gown and slide inside the thin cotton of her nightdress and find the eager tilt of her breast. Even with his lips on her, colour flooded Jenna's face. She knew why he was doing this and she knew too that this was an intimacy she had never permitted before in her life. She was ashamed of the swollen evidence his fingers sought and found, but there was nothing she could do to wrench herself free. It was like a drug, like the swell of the ocean, and she went down under the waves.

'Gently, *chérie*.' When he lifted her she could hear her own panic-stricken murmurings and he pulled her head against him, muffling the wild little sounds against the strength of his neck. Even as he carried her out of the lighted kitchen his lips continued to caress her and she was not in any way close to recovering as he placed her on her feet in her own room. She had no memory of any stairs. She could only feel what Alain had made her feel.

As she swayed dizzily he caught her, stripping off her dressing-gown and placing her in bed. He bent to kiss her and before she could recover he had pulled the sheets over her and walked out, closing the door and going down the stairs as softly as he had come up. Jenna lay in a daze, her whole being shaken. He had demanded submission and she had submitted very willingly.

She turned her hot face into the pillows and tried to get some sort of control over her heartbeats. Downstairs, Alain was walking about, switching off lights, locking the door, and for a wild moment she thought he would come back here to her. When he finally walked past her room to go to his she was ashamed and shocked at the disappointment that raced through her. He had said that she had potential, but she had not known how much.

Glyn never made her feel like this, he never even tried. Deep inside she knew that if he had tried she would have repulsed him, and she looked out of the window at the moonlit sky. Just what sort of a marriage was she planning for herself? A shudder raced through her as self-knowledge hit her hard. She had wanted Alain to come back. What sort of a person did that make her? What sort of a person did it make Alain when he would behave like that because he had suffered a frustrating evening.

In the morning he was once again out and Marguerite was not her cheerful self.

'I imagine he has gone to say goodbye to Claudine,' she announced, although Jenna had not dared to ask where he was. She didn't want to see him although she knew perfectly well that he would have to be faced. 'He is not in the best of moods this morning,' Marguerite continued. 'Perhaps they quarrelled last night? Who knows? Whatever happened, I seem to be suffering for it. He flatly refuses to allow me to stay here alone.'

She said nothing more and Jenna sat down to her breakfast, but as she glanced across at Marguerite, who was busy at the cooker, she saw tears standing in the dark eyes and guilt rushed over her as she realised why. If she felt the presence of a man she had never known here in this house, just how much did Marguerite feel his presence and just how much did she need it at this time?

Nothing was healed. For her things would never heal, but for Marguerite time would lessen the pain and her memories would help. The memories all seemed to be here in the Dordogne and Alain must know it. For a moment she felt anger at his unfeeling attitude, but common sense prevailed. He was right. This house was isolated, no place for a woman alone. When they left for Paris, Marguerite would have to go with them. She would even worry about his mother herself if she stayed alone, so how much more would Alain worry? He was not allowing it because he could not.

He came back in the middle of the morning and his eyes met Jenna's at once. She refused to be cowardly and hang her head. However badly she had behaved last night, he was worse. His eyes were black and expressionless and he gave her no more than one probing glance before turning away.

'I suggest that you both pack,' he said abruptly. 'It is a long journey. We will eat lunch on the way.'

'Oh, Alain! I have already started to prepare it,' Marguerite protested. 'I have *coq au vin* in the oven right now.'

'*Maman*, you did this deliberately.' He sighed wearily and ran his hand through his hair. 'Believe me, I know how you feel, but I must take account of your safety. I dare not leave you here alone.'

'She won't be alone,' Jenna said quickly, rushing the words out before good sense got the better of her. 'I'll stay for a few days at least—if she can put up with me.'

'Oh, Jenna! I need you!' Marguerite flung her arms around Jenna and hugged her. 'But are you sure? Don't you have to go back to that school of yours?'

'I can spare a few days,' Jenna assured her, not daring to look at Alain. 'I've got indefinite leave—it's not a state school, and I'm lucky that the head is a very sympathetic woman, even though she is a little odd.'

'So you will stay? I accept. Now, Alain. Is that all right for you?'

Marguerite turned on Alain and he managed a tight smile.

'*Naturellement*. You have your companion. I can leave you with an easy mind.'

'Then off you go, both of you. Out of my kitchen.' She shooed them away happily, but Jenna was anything but happy. Pity for Alain's mother had driven her to this gesture and she knew she would regret it. Safety lay in England. Still, she would have done her bit and her conscience would be clear. She walked straight through the sitting-room and out into the sunshine. She wanted no probing questions from Alain. She wanted no thanks, no suspicious questions, and she most certainly did not want to get close to that hard, sensuous mouth.

She hadn't gone far when Alain joined her, and he simply matched his pace to suit her own, saying nothing at all. She was breathlessly aware of him and she walked across to the fence that faced the field she could see from her room and stood there looking out into the distance. Now that she had offered to stay she was almost panic-stricken by her own actions. It would mean seeing Alain again and she wasn't sure if she could do that and retain any distance.

'Whenever you wish to get out of here I will come and fetch you,' he said quietly. 'I am well aware that you have no real desire to stay.'

'There were tears in your mother's eyes this morning. She needs to be where he was—at least for a little while.' She felt she must make sure he knew why she was doing this—for Marguerite alone and not because she seemed to be unable to resist when he held her.

'I know,' he assured her sombrely. 'Even so, she is my responsibility and I could not have left her here alone.'

'I know.' Jenna nodded, her eyes on the field, trying to imagine it full of poppies and trying to keep her mind off Alain. It was the first time she had been alone with him since last night and the thought of it made her fluttery inside.

'Are there poppies in this field?' she asked shakily.

'Yes. Each year. You are imagining them?'

'Did he paint them?'

'Yes. Twice, as far as I can remember. One of the paintings is in the studio. He never did get around to framing it.' He made an impatient movement and faced her, looking at her pure profile. 'You are changing the subject very purposefully. Are you afraid I will thank you for your generous gesture towards my mother?'

'It's not so generous,' Jenna lied. 'I like your mother and I knew she badly wanted to stay.'

'Perhaps not as badly as you wished to go,' he interrupted harshly.

'I'm not so desperate now. After all, I looked at the paintings. . .'

'And fled from the studio.'

'I could face it now,' Jenna said determinedly. 'This week I'll go up there.'

The statement brought an unexpected reaction.

'Not without me!' He took her shoulders and spun her to face him. 'When you go up there, I go with you.'

'If you think I'd damage anything either deliberately or accidently. . .'

'I do not. That is not the reason for the order.'

'Maybe your mother will go with me, then.' Jenna could not understand his attitude and looked up at him with wide, puzzled eyes. That did not satisfy him either.

'No! She is not ready to face that. Just leave it, Jenna. I do not have time to take you there now. Next time I come. . .'

'Look, I'm not so anxious to go up there. Forget all about it. If you're in a hurry to go then why waste your time talking to me?'

'You are not a waste of time, Jenna.' His mood changed like quicksilver, the sombreness vanishing as if it had never been there. 'Besides, now that I do not have to stop on the way to Paris for lunch I can go later. Without my two passengers I will also go faster.'

'You want to be careful,' Jenna said seriously. 'I thought you came fast enough on the way here.'

'Ah! You would care if I had an accident?' He was back to teasing again and Jenna's serious looks changed to flustered annoyance.

'I was thinking about your mother,' she snapped. 'She's had enough grief. Then again there's Claudine,' she added spitefully. 'I was thinking about her too.'

He grasped her chin in one hand and tilted it to meet her angry eyes.

'You were not thinking about her last night, *petite*,' he taunted. 'You were not thinking about your lawyer friend either.'

Jenna tried to jerk her face from his grasp, but he tightened his hold, refusing to let her go.

'You're quite despicable, aren't you?' she said fiercely, keeping to anger to disguise her uneven breathing and her warmly flushed face.

'I am? May I remind you that I let you go? I even helped you to bed and did not demand to stay with you.'

'How dare you speak like this? Just because you have such a high opinion of your prowess. . .'

'I have a high opinion of my mother,' he corrected with a dark, mocking smile. He let her go and ran a long finger across her cheek. 'You were gentle, warm and willing but my mother was in the house. Perhaps, next time, she will not be there.'

'You're trying to make me go, aren't you?' Jenna whispered fiercely. By now her cheeks were flaming and he looked at her with an almost analytical expression on his face.

'*Pas question*! I am telling you that last night I wanted you. Any normal girl would have known, of course, but with you one cannot be certain. You are unaccustomed to passion. This morning you are quite safe.' He suddenly stopped teasing. 'Do not go for lonely walks while I am away.'

'I'll be safer with Bernard than with you, if that's what you mean!' Jenna snapped, spinning away and storming off towards the house. He caught her in two strides and his expression was neither analytical nor taunting. He was annoyed.

'Do not believe that for one second,' he grated. 'If I imagined you were about to repeat your foolishness of the other day I would insist that you came back to Paris now. I will mention it to my mother. She must take care of you.'

'Oh, stop it!' Jenna raged. 'I'm staying of my own free will to allow your mother to stay. Apart from that I do as I like. Nobody orders me about.'

She pulled free and walked off and this time he let her go. When he came into the house she was reading a book she had brought with her and she didn't even look up. Alain carefully ignored her until it was time to go and she watched his car sweep from the house with very mixed feelings. She told herself she was glad to see the back of him, but it was not strictly true. Also, she was now trapped here until he decided to come and fetch her, and she knew she would miss him daily.

With Marguerite she settled into an amiable routine. The sun made it warm enough to sit outside and, although swimming in the pool was out of the question so early in the year, Jenna managed to get an even golden tan. She gained a few necessary pounds in weight too, and it was all due to the quiet and calm of the house, Marguerite's soothing presence and an entirely unexpected sense of peace and belonging.

Gradually she wheedled her way into the kitchen and began to learn the art of French cooking from Alain's mother, and what with one thing and another she hardly noticed the days pass by. There was just one thing to cause her unease. Each day she listened for Alain's return. It was entirely against her will and utterly ridiculous, but she could not seem to stop doing it.

Reluctantly she admitted that she wanted to see him all the time. It was the only thing that made her restless, and Marguerite noticed.

'Today is Thursday,' she commented one morning. 'We have been here alone since Sunday. I expect it is time to venture out before you get bored.'

'Oh, I'm not bored,' Jenna put in quickly. 'I've even forgotten all about school,' she added with a guilty smile. 'At this rate I won't have a job to go back to.'

'Really? You gave all this up to stay with me?' Alain's mother looked guilty herself and Jenna hurried to correct her.

'I've not given anything up. I'm enjoying it. Look at me. You can see how much better I am.'

'You look quite healthy now,' Marguerite agreed. 'All the same, how long can you stay before you lose this job of yours?'

'Maybe one more week.' In fact, there was no chance of losing her job, but sooner or later she would have to go and it seemed a good idea to lay down a time now. That way Marguerite would not be disappointed.

'Then we must make the most of it,' she said briskly. 'I have some shopping to do and you have not been to the town at all. We'll go immediately after breakfast.'

'On foot?' Jenna looked at her wryly. The nearest town was some distance away and Alain had driven off in the car.

'*Mais non*! I have a car here. As far as I know it works as well as ever.'

The car in question was a little Renault, and Jenna was interested as Marguerite led her to the garage later and opened it up. Apparently it was also a general storehouse for things from the house, and by the wall was a bicycle.

'That is Alain's,' Marguerite said as Jenna inspected it with interest. 'It must be years since he has ridden it. He is not so light-hearted now as he used to be—too much responsibility. There was a time, though, when every weekend he would be off on that cycle. It is not a thing for the amateur,' she added warningly as Jenna eyed it with glee. 'It is a fast racing machine.'

Jenna could see that it was, but she made a note to sneak in here when she had a minute and try it out. It was years since she had ridden a bike too, not since she had been at school and had cycled home each day. The thought came into her mind that, while she had been doing that, Alain had been here, going out on his splendid machine, coming home to talk to his mother and to *her* father. The picture was clearly in her head, but it brought none of the old bitterness, because now she was seeing Alain, imagining him, and it wiped away the old grief. It was true—walls were crumbling and she had better make sure that new ones were not built. Especially ones she could not scale. Her cheeks grew pink at the thought of even trying and Marguerite looked at her curiously, mistaking her expression.

'I do not suppose that Alain would be annoyed it you

tried out his old cycle,' she said quickly. 'I only meant that it would not be suitable to go on the road with it. You would need perhaps more skill than you have.'

'I'm sure I would.' Jenna grinned at her and got into the car, looking around with pleasure as Marguerite reversed from the garage and turned to the track. The old house was once again golden and mellow in the sun. Daily the heat grew and daily she felt more and more reluctant to leave here.

She was making peace with herself and with her father and suddenly she wanted to tell Alain, to thank him for forcing this on her. Bitterness ate into the soul and at last her soul was clearing, calming. With a guilty start she remembered she had not phoned Glyn since Paris.

'When we come back I must phone home,' she told Marguerite.

'Of course, *ma chère*, whenever you want to.'

Jenna smiled and sank into silence. The word 'home' just didn't seem to ring true any more. For now she was torn between two places and it was not the thought of her father that bound her to this place. It was the chance that she would see Alain, that he would suddenly come with his dark, sardonic smiles, his caustic comments and his unexpected kisses.

They turned south this time and soon Jenna was amused and intrigued to see huge gaggles of geese in fields, moving about almost as one and honking loud enough to be heard over the noise of the car.

'The geese make much noise,' Marguerite remarked, frowning at them as she sped past. 'They are also often quite fierce.'

'I've never seen so many,' Jenna remarked, turning in her seat to look back.

'This is *foie gras* country. The district produces tons of the pâté. Each concern is family run, but it produces one of our greatest culinary delights.'

It rather wiped the smile from Jenna's face. Her

English mind could not contemplate the force-feeding of these geese, no matter how fierce they were.

'There are also truffles here. You know what they are?'

'A sort of underground fungus?' Jenna made a wry face, and Marguerite laughed at her expression.

'*Ma chère*, they are wonderful and *so* expensive! They have a very distinctive taste and are not to be wasted by offering them to an indifferent chef to prepare.'

It led Marguerite on to the art of cooking, and Jenna was content to sit and listen to the soothing sound of her voice. Now that Marguerite was confident with her, her English had surfaced again. No doubt she had spoken English with Russell and it was all coming back to her.

The town was small and neat, typical of the towns of the area, almost all of it built around the central square, which was shaded by high trees. Jenna wanted to roam off by herself and do a little window-gazing, but Marguerite took her arm in a surprisingly strong grip.

'No! If anything should happen to you, Alain would be furious with me. We have just got you well again, Jenna, and I cannot take the responsibility of letting you out of my sight.'

'I'm not a child!' Jenna laughed. 'I'm quite capable of taking care of myself.'

'You do not speak French,' Marguerite said triumphantly, and Jenna had to agree. *When* would people stop taking care of her? They had never even tried it until she had first seen Alain and now it seemed that every step she took was to be supervised.

'I came to France alone, you know,' she pointed out firmly, but Alain's mother had her there too.

'But Alain was waiting for you, *n'est-ce pas*? He instructed me to look after you,' she finished with a look that said it was no use arguing.

'He probably thinks I'm an imbecile,' Jenna muttered frustratedly.

'He thinks you are a little delicate,' Marguerite said

comfortably, leading her to a stall in the open-air market that was well stocked with bright fruit and fresh vegetables. 'It is your colouring, dear. Alain has always been intrigued by your colouring.'

'Always?' Jenna looked at her in astonishment, but there was no reply. Marguerite was testing and discarding fruit and vegetables with an almost fanatical zeal. The great French cook was buying in supplies and Jenna knew not to interrupt. If Alain had been intrigued by her colouring since he had first seen her then why hadn't Marguerite said so? 'Always' was an odd choice of word, denoting a great length of time. It was probably the translation.

CHAPTER EIGHT

IN SPITE of being almost tethered to Marguerite, Jenna enjoyed the trip and was rewarded later by being instructed in the cooking of some of the purchases. Happily there was no pâté de *foie gras* to alarm her and certainly no truffles to cook. Even her call to Glyn had been successful. He was back to his old ways, quiet and undemanding, and he admitted that he was missing her badly.

'How long is this thing going to take, Jenna?' he wanted to know. 'It's pretty dull here without you. Funny thing, I hadn't noticed before what a one-horse town this was. I hadn't noticed what a weird old bird Ned was, either. I'm beginning to feel like a Martian here without you. I've even been past Grey House twice to see if by any chance your car was there, to see if you'd come back and not let me know. Silly, really,' he added in embarrassment.

'It's not silly if you're missing me,' Jenna said soothingly. 'I'm missing you too.' When she had said that before she had meant it, but now she realised she was lying; she was wanting to make him feel better and she was also hanging on to her old life to feel safe. She knew perfectly well why. Her thoughts were far too much on Alain and it was quite ridiculous. This was a business arrangement and nothing more. Whatever Alain's plans, they did not include her, other than her enabling him to see his mother happily back in charge of her own home. As to the kisses, hadn't he said it was because he was French? Perhaps they didn't take things to heart so much.

'I'll be back in a week,' she told Glyn firmly.

'We'll get engaged.' As he rang off after this unexpected statement, Jenna felt again the old familiar tightening around her heart, the trapped feeling, and the memory of Alain's arms came surging back into her mind. Having felt like that with Alain, how would she feel with Glyn? Was she about to risk the rest of her life for safety?

She was pleasantly sleepy by bedtime in spite of her thoughts and for once had a dreamless sleep, no images of her mother to distract and disturb her. Now it was Alain's face that surfaced when she let down her guard.

Her last thought was to wonder what life would have been like had she been here with her father instead of in England with her mother. She would have grown up with Marguerite's calm influence around her; she would have been more French than English. She would have been close to Alain. It was all so much useless speculation because, when everything was truly laid out sensibly, her father had not wanted her.

Next morning Jenna inspected the garage and determinedly got out the bike. In the sunlight she could see that it was indeed a rather splendid machine. She dusted it off and then rather timidly mounted it. The fact that it was a man's bike didn't trouble her too much. She was wearing trousers and as she kept her feet on the ground she felt reasonably secure, at least; she kept her toes on the ground and spent a rather hilarious time trying to get control of it in the courtyard, her attempts bringing Marguerite out with words of advice and wide smiles.

When Alain's mother finally went inside with a few rueful shakes of her head and a pleased look on her face, Jenna decided to risk all. She set off boldly towards the fence and only had to put her feet down speedily once. After her third attempt she felt quite secure and rather smug. Not smug enough, however, to tackle the track.

It was not the thought of a fall that worried her. As far as she knew, Marie would be here today, and she had no intention of making a fool of herself and allowing the girl more gossip to tell Claudine. The field in front of the house was reasonably flat and she set off to tackle that. No doubt she would be doing the cycle irreparable damage, but the urge to ride it was too strong to be denied.

She lifted it over the fence and set off across the little meadow, gathering speed and thoroughly enjoying it. The gears were tricky and elaborate, but she managed them after one or two mistakes, and by the time she had been round once she felt very proud of herself. The whole morning became encapsulated in the smell of grass, the sound of the tyres and the wind blowing her hair as she went faster and faster.

Coming back round by the house for the third time, she got quite above herself, and the bike began to wobble alarmingly as she fought to control it. Failing miserably, she found herself sliding sideways, and there was nothing she could do but laugh as she hit the field quite hard and bike landed on top of her. It didn't hurt. Nothing could have hurt on this glorious morning and she had quite forgotten about Marie and the amusement the girl would have had in seeing her.

It was not Marie who saw her. Jenna lay looking at the sky, breathing in the smell of the grass and smiling to herself. She didn't even bother to move the bike. It was not heavy at all and moving would have been just too much effort. Contentment filled her and she watched the high white clouds.

She only became aware of her rather foolish escapade when she found Alain towering over her, looking down at her with narrowed, amused eyes, his lips quirking very close to open laughter.

'Not spectacular, but well worth seeing,' he observed. He stood with his hands in his pockets and she realised she had been so taken up with her seemingly childish pursuit that she had not even heard the car arrive.

'It's only Friday,' she muttered, staring up at him, her hand shading her eyes from the sun.

'They let me out from time to time,' he stated seriously. All the time his eyes were laughing down at her and she suddenly flushed when she realised how she must look, lying there on the grass.

At her first move to get up he leaned over and lifted the bike from her, but before she could get to her feet he was beside her, sitting on the grass and looking down into her flushed face.

'I suppose I shouldn't have got the bike out,' she began uneasily.

'I don't mind.' He shrugged lazily. 'I am not saving it for the Tour de France. Perhaps you could enter, though? I watched your last circuit of the field.'

'I suppose I've ruined the bike on this grass,' she insisted. She didn't want to get up. After all the waiting for him he was here so unexpectedly, and she admitted that she simply wanted to look at him.

'I will add it to the account when you leave,' he murmured. Their eyes held for a long time and then he rested back on his elbows and looked at the treetops, his face suddenly serious. 'I have been in already to see my mother. You have made her happy, Jenna, given her something to hang on to.'

'I've enjoyed it,' she admitted. 'Unfortunately I have to leave soon.'

'Why?' He turned his head and looked down into her face. 'Why do you have to leave? You do not seem to be unhappy.'

'I have a job and—and Glyn is missing me.'

'Is he?' He frowned rather alarmingly and Jenna felt a burst of nerves coming on; she moved to get up but found herself being pushed back relentlessly. 'Stay right there,' he ordered. 'We will talk this out.'

'There's nothing at all to talk out. I can stay another

week; after that I must go. I *do* have a home in England and I have a job. Life can't be one long holiday.'

He relaxed on the grass beside her, staring up at the sky.

'I suppose not,' he sighed frustratedly. 'All the same, I have not done what I set out to do. Nothing is different at all.'

'But it is!' Jenna sat up and looked down at him eagerly. 'You've no idea how different I feel. All the bitterness seems to have gone. I feel so comfortable with your mother and the whole time here has changed me for the better.'

He lifted his hand and trailed a lazy finger across her cheek. 'What about the ghosts?'

'Still there, I suppose.' Jenna looked across towards the barn and then flung herself back beside him to lie watching the clouds scudding across the blue sky. 'I can face it, I imagine, but I don't know what the result will be. Maybe I'll lose this—this feeling I've gained here. Maybe I'll be bitter again.'

'*Peut-être.*' He sat up and leaned over her. 'You will never know until you try.' When she just looked up at him he cupped her face in his hand. 'You want to try, Jenna?'

'I don't know.'

For a moment he stroked her fair hair back away from her face, his eyes roaming over her, and Jenna could hear her own heart beating like a hammer. It was ridiculous how she felt about Alain. Nothing could come of it. She was just asking for further grief. Their eyes held for a moment and a slow smile began to grow on the darkly handsome face.

'I will really have to do something drastic about you, Jenna Bryant.'

He stood swiftly and pulled her to her feet, steadying her as she swayed. She felt light-headed and it was not just the swift change from lying down to standing. It was

Alain's presence, his powerful personality, his devastating masculinity. The way she felt about him seemed to sweep round her like the clouds up above.

'You are afraid of losing what you have gained here?' he asked softly, holding her arms. 'Is it so good?'

'Good enough to hang on to,' she whispered, staring up at him. 'I might be right back where I started.'

'Not really.' He suddenly smiled down at her. 'If one wants something badly enough, the will to cling to it is very strong.' His eyes skimmed over her face, his gaze arrested at her softly parted lips, and Jenna looked down, afraid of what she was feeling.

'I'm light-headed,' she muttered, colour flooding her cheeks.

'So am I,' he said drily, turning her to the house. 'We are probably allergic to grass.' He bent and scooped up the bike, wheeling it along with them, and Jenna became aware of other eyes besides the dark ones that had looked into her own. Marie had arrived and she was watching openly, making no move to go into the house and get on with her job. Another tale to tell, more speculation.

Alain ignored it. He behaved as if he hadn't seen Marie, and the girl went into the house when Jenna stared at her forcefully.

'I suggest we have coffee and then consider the problem,' Alain murmured. 'We will face the barn or we will go out somewhere.'

'But you've just driven from Paris! Surely you're tired?'

'I was,' he assured her wryly. 'Somehow, though, watching you racing round the field like a schoolgirl has given me a burst of energy. We could go out to lunch,' he offered.

Jenna's heady feeling died quickly.

'I'm not going to the château!' she announced forcefully.

'You do not like it? Or perhaps it is Claudine you do

not like?' He shot her a glittering glance, but Jenna was ready for him.

'Definitely the château. It's cold and dark, as I said before, and I prefer Marguerite's cooking. As to Claudine, I never thought about her. I don't know her and don't expect to. After next week there'll be no chance whatever of seeing her again.'

'So, you will never come back? You like my mother and yet you will be content to dismiss her from your life?' He stopped at the fence and looked down at her seriously.

'Not content, no. But how can I. . .?'

'How can you see her without seeing me? I am the one you wish to avoid, *n'est-ce pas*?'

'I—I don't really mind you. . .' Jenna began awkwardly, and he suddenly gave a shout of laughter, vaulting the fence and then reaching to lift her over as if she weighed nothing at all.

'Perhaps I *mind* you, my intriguing little near-relative?' he laughed. He was still holding her in the loose circle of his arms and she instantly bridled at the teasing.

'I'm not. . .!' she began hotly, but his finger came swiftly to her lips, stopping the outburst.

'You are not a relative?' he murmured helpfully. 'I agree. I would not have felt such a burst of passion for a relative.'

'You were obviously drunk,' Jenna snapped, blushing hotly.

'Certainly I was light-headed,' he agreed smoothly. 'So were you, *petite*, very light-headed.'

'It's not gentlemanly to talk like this,' Jenna pointed out primly.

'But I am not a gentleman like you lawyer friend, *chérie*. Neither am I an imbecile.'

'You can let me go now,' Jenna said stiffly, reminding him that he was still holding her in arms that were beginning to tighten almost imperceptibly.

'I beg your pardon,' he said mockingly. 'I quite forgot that you don't like it.' He reached over the fence and collected the bike and Jenna looked at it gloomily.

'You've taken away all my calm assurance,' she burst out with painful honesty.

'Did you expect otherwise? My mother gave you the calm. I merely make you angry.' He suddenly grinned at her, taking her arm. 'Perhaps I have not been trying hard enough. Forgive me, Jenna. You are sometimes so stiffly English that you bring out the need to tease. I will take care in future.'

'When—when I go back—next week,' Jenna said in a rush before they reached the house, 'will you come to collect me or do you want me to get to Paris by myself?'

'Naturally I will collect both of you.' From laughter he was instantly grim. 'My mother cannot stay here alone. It will not be possible to get a housekeeper to her satisfaction immediately. She will stay with me.'

'I'm sorry,' Jenna muttered.

'It is not your fault,' he said coldly, no trace of the gently teasing man left. 'Our life went its own way before you came. No doubt it will go its own way when you have gone.'

They went inside and Marie's knowing looks seemed to infuriate Alain even more. He snapped at her.

'Kindly clean upstairs,' he ordered, no matter what his mother had asked her to do. 'We are about to have coffee here. You may finish here later.'

'*Oui, monsieur*.' She scuttled off and when Jenna looked up Marguerite was watching from the doorway to the kitchen. She simply went back in there and was out again very swiftly with coffee for two. If she was having any herself, she was not about to join them. No doubt she could see the danger signs when things displeased her powerful son. She must have had to duck when Alain's father was displeased too, Jenna thought sourly, frowning at Alain.

'There's no need to be annoyed with your mother,' she pointed out crossly.

'I am never annoyed with my mother,' he grated. 'You are the irritation, *mademoiselle*, and, on this occasion, also that vacuous Marie.'

'She'll hear you!' Jenna whispered in a shocked voice.

'*Bien*! Then she will know more than she did as she went up the stairs, my little English mouse. Try saying what is in your heart instead of being so timid.'

'Very well,' Jenna snapped. 'You're overbearing, impolite and arrogant!'

'I can only agree,' he muttered derisively. 'That being the case, come to the barn.' He drained his coffee and stood to tower over her and she glared up at him.

'If you insist! See if I care!'

'What a child you are,' he taunted. 'Even your language is like a schoolgirl.'

'I'm an English graduate!' Jenna stormed, brushing past him on her way to the door.

'But so immature,' he murmured ironically.

'You're goading me on purpose!' She spun round to glare at him and found him much too close, his eyes burning down at her.

'Perhaps I am,' he agreed. 'Perhaps I am hoping that temper will sustain you through this ordeal. I have seen your temper help you out on several occasions.'

Time will tell, Jenna thought. Faced with actually going back to the barn, she was not now so serene about it as she had been when she was lying in the field and gazing at the sky. She glanced at the sky now but quickly looked away. How swiftly she and Alain came to temper. It was quite sad. Still, he was a stranger after all. His life was not like hers and she was simply an outsider who had been forced to come here. Soon she would go and he would forget all about her, except perhaps for those wry little moments when he would remember her childish temper and smile to himself in his superior way.

This time there was no need for him to force her up the dark steps of the barn; she walked in front of him determinedly. Nothing could upset her here. She told herself that very firmly, and when Alain swung the door to the studio wide to allow her to enter Jenna walked in without hesitation. She was ready now for the sight of the chair, the pipe, the feeling that her father had only popped out for a minute and would be back before she could leave.

This time too she walked around the room and studied the paintings. Many were still unframed and she had to admit that she loved them. The colours, the form and intense feeling of light and pleasure wee exactly her own taste. It was odd to think that even without his talent she had inherited this from her father.

There were two easels, one with an unfinished picture of a town and the other holding a painting on a large canvas, but it was not possible to see it. A dark cloth had been thrown over it, covering it completely.

'What's that?' She looked at Alain and waited for his permission to uncover the painting. So far she had felt very little because she had been well prepared, but she did not have the necessary audacity to simply whisk the cloth away. This was somehow still Alain's task, still his right.

'That is why you are here, Jenna,' he said softly. 'This will tell you all you wish to know. It will speak the truth and straighten the record. The painting on the easel is a portrait. It was finished many years ago and has never been moved since. He sat in that chair and looked at it as he rested. Stand over there and see what he saw every day.'

He looked steadily at her and Jenna moved back obediently, her heart suddenly pounding with anxiety because she had no idea what Alain was talking about. She only knew that he was very serious and that this was important to him for some reason. He pulled the cloth away and Jenna made no sound at all although her cheeks went quite pale.

It was a young girl on a bicycle, the feeling of movement captured easily. Silver-gilt hair flowed behind her, clear eyes looked out at the world and her fresh skin was tinted with delicate colour. Long, slender legs showed beneath the swirling pleats of a school skirt. The striped tie was neat beneath the collar of a white blouse. Even the badge on the dark blazer was faithfully recorded.

'It's me.' Jenna whispered the words, her eyes never leaving the image of what she had been long ago. She saw the wistful eyes, the carefully contained emotion, and the long, lost years came rushing back to choke her.

'Yes. It is you.' Alain stood by the picture and read the words of dedication by her father's signature. '"Jenna at sixteen". It is certainly you. He treasured it until he died.'

'And yet he never wanted me. How could he have known what I looked like? It's not possible.'

'It is possible, Jenna. He had a photograph. I took it and I still have it.' He glanced at her woebegone face, his eyes intent and probing. 'He wanted you, Jenna. He wanted his daughter more than anything in the world.'

'He never even came to see me, never wrote. Don't try to deceive me, Alain. There's nothing but sadness here.' She turned away and covered her face with trembling hands. 'Can I go now?'

'Yes,' he said heavily. 'If you cannot see beyond the painted image, beyond the obvious, then perhaps you should go, perhaps you should have never even come.'

'I never wanted to. Is this what you promised me—roots laid down for me in France? A portrait from a photograph?'

'The roots are love,' he said sharply. 'They are here if you will listen.'

'What love? There never was any!' She spun round to face him with blazing blue eyes and then her head fell as the blue became blurred with tears, and pity for herself, for her mother and for the man she scarcely remembered came flooding with the tears that fell down her cheeks. 'I—I suppose I'm childish?'

'No, Jenna. Things from childhood live with us for the rest of our lives. Perhaps if you had been a different sort of person—less sensitive, less driven by the bitterness of your mother. . .'

'She had good reason!' Jenna lifted her head angrily but the tears still fell, out of her control, and with a murmur of frustration Alain strode forwards and pulled her into his arms.

He pushed her head to his shoulder and she found herself snuggling into the comfort, relaxing as his hand stroked through her hair. He rocked her in warmth, holding her close until the harsh sobbing eased. Her tears were wetting his shirt and she lifted her hand, wiping at her wet cheeks and smoothing the white shirt thoughtlessly, trying to make it dry. Her fingers felt the warmth of his skin through the silk of the shirt and innocently lingered over the heavy beat of his heart.

She was startled when he took her hand impatiently and moved it and some small hurt must have shown on her face at his swift action because he looked down at her frustratedly.

'Sometimes, your actions are utterly thoughtless without any knowledge of consequences,' he muttered, turning her to the side of the room, where a long bench gave them a chance to sit. Whether she wanted to or not she was facing the portrait and Alain looked at it too, his expression sombre.

'It is how I first saw you,' he confessed grimly. 'I took the photograph and I wanted to stride across to you, to confront you with your father, but he would not allow it.'

'I—I don't understand any of this.' Jenna looked up at him with tear-drenched eyes and he wiped them almost absently, his mind clearly in the past.

'How could you?' he asked with a bitterness of his own. 'Nobody would tell you.' He removed his arm from her shoulders and leaned back against the wall, his gaze still on the fair-haired young girl who sat on the bicycle, ready to move off, the wind blowing her skirt and hair. 'I have often wondered why the nervy, fastidious Imogen married Russell,' he mused grimly. 'He was an artist, not particularly tidy, too dreamy to match her ways. Did you know he gave up what he wanted to do so that you could have material comforts?' Jenna looked up at him and shook her head and he looked abruptly away, back to the girl who seemed almost real. 'He was not well known then and he put his desires aside to take commercial artwork. It was soul-destroying to him but it gave him money for his wife and child. He painted when he could—in his little spare time, in his holidays. Imogen refused to go with him and would not allow you to either.'

He suddenly stood, leaving her, pacing about before spinning to face her determinedly.

'There was another man, Jenna.' At the look on her face he held up his hand, silencing her ready protests. 'It is nothing you can deny,' he informed her sharply. 'You were too young to know.'

'Ned Clarke, the—the solicitor said she started the divorce proceedings,' Jenna confessed.

'She did, and Russell was so unhappy that he did not contest it.' Alain sat down by her again, turning her to face him. 'What he did *not* agree to was losing you!' he said harshly. 'That part of the divorce was all very amicable on the surface. He was to have access to his daughter whenever possible. They were both agreed that you should not be dragged into things. You were eight years old and I suppose it is to your mother's credit that she wanted to spare you any court proceedings. At any rate, her attitude fooled Russell completely. She got the house and contents, the car and all the money in the bank. Even though he knew there was somebody else,

Russell gave up his claim to anything so that he could see you, have you to stay with him, keep his daughter, and Imogen graciously agreed.'

'But my father never did try to see me,' Jenna said miserably. She was startled at the savagery of Alain's reaction to this mild statement.

'He tried for eight years!' he rasped.

'He never even wrote.'

'I think he wrote a little to you every single day for those eight years, posted the thick, heavy letters when you were found again. Have you no imagination, Jenna? Have you not wondered about it? What do you think happened to the letters that came to any house you lived in?'

'My mother always collected the mail.' She looked up at him and then shook her head. 'It's no use, Alain. He could have got a court order. He could have come and demanded to see me, sat on the doorstep.'

'If he had been able to find the doorstep! Listen to me, Jenna! As soon as the divorce was settled and your mother was free, she moved. Russell had given up everything and he came to France, where he had friends. He came to start again, to build a home he could bring you to, even if only for your holidays. Immediately, your mother disappeared and took you with her. The house was sold, the bank account closed, and nobody knew where she was. He got court orders, but what were they? They were merely bits of paper. She had done nothing criminal; she had merely broken a sworn promise. Many court orders are ignored. All it takes is the necessary nerve, and Imogen had plenty of that.'

'But he found me eventually. . .'

'No. *I* found you!' Alain looked more grim than ever, but his looks softened as he glanced down at her white face. 'At first, after he married my mother, I was too busy and not even completely interested. I was at university and then learning the business I had inherited. As I got to know Russell I began to be angry at this woman who was still causing him misery. I too wanted to trace her, to see the lost Jenna. I tracked your mother down. I was then well able to afford help and I employed private detectives. Even they had trouble because she covered her tracks very well. When I knew for sure where you were I came to England alone. I waited by the house and I saw you come home from school. The last man I had hired came with me and assured me that the girl who rode to the house was Jenna Bryant. You stopped to talk to a friend and that was when I photographed you.'

'So why didn't my father come then?' Jenna asked wearily, looking down at her clenched hands.

'He came. I brought him two days later and he saw you. We were in a car I hired. We watched you come home, we saw you go into the house and I was all for going right in after you and confronting Imogen, telling you the truth, because I had learned all about how she had dragged you from place to place, from house to house. My detectives had established your many moves and it did not take much intelligence to realise why.' He sighed and leaned back against the wall again. 'Russell stopped me. He said you were sixteen now, your life settled. He felt he could only be an unwelcome addition to your life. I even remember his words. "Leave her in peace, Alain. If she's suffered at all then it will be over now. I have no right to start it again. Imogen will simply move off to another place." It was useless to tell him that you were grown-up enough to have a mind of your own now. He didn't want to intrude into your life. He came back here and started the portrait. It seemed to have more life than the photograph.'

Jenna said nothing. Her mind was too busy seeing the man who had wearily let her go, not wilfully, as she had always imagined, but finally, for what he thought was her own good.

'And I never even came to see him when he was dying,' she choked.

'You had an accident,' he reminded her.

'Maybe I wouldn't have come in any case.' Jenna was filled with misery and still puzzled by so many things. Guilt too was eating at her. 'He died knowing that I wouldn't come,' she whispered.

'No, he did not,' Alain said, his arm coming round her comfortingly again. 'I thought it necessary to lie a little. When you did not phone in answer to my letter, I told him that you were overseas. I told him the letter had been posted on to you and it was merely a matter of time before you got it.'

'He didn't have any time,' Jenna reminded him unhappily.

'I knew that,' Alain confessed. 'Russell did not know it. He died happily, Jenna; everyone who loved him was around him. He was waiting to see you and fully expecting you would be there. As it happened, it was for the best. You did not understand then and things might have been awkward.'

Jenna just nodded. Now the tears moved no further than the back of her eyes. Her father had been happy, had friends, had this wonderful talent. Alain pulled her head to his shoulder and they both gazed at the portrait.

'Pretty young girl on a bike,' Alain mused softly. 'I saw her again this morning as she rode round the field. This time, though, she looked happy.' He tilted her face and looked into her eyes. 'Were you happy, Jenna?'

'I suppose I was—for a while.'

Alain continued to look down at her, his eyes moving over her upturned face, and then he stood abruptly and motioned to the door.

'Let us go back to the house. It must be almost time for lunch.'

'But there's so much more I want to know. . .'

'Later,' he said stiffly. 'I think we have been in this place long enough.'

CHAPTER NINE

SOMEHOW Jenna felt she had offended Alain, but she couldn't imagine how. When he opened the door for her she stepped out towards the dark stairs of the barn, her mind still in the bright, airy room, and at the top of the steps she suddenly swayed giddily, pitching towards the stairs.

'Alain!' There really had been no need to call to him. His arms were around her as his name left her lips.

'You are faint?' Alain held her and she flushed softly, feeling all manner of a fool.

'No, really I'm not. I think it was the sudden transition from light to dark.'

'I will go down first, then.' He still sounded cross and Jenna bit her lip, looking up at him worriedly.

'I know that in some way I've offended you,' she began. 'I didn't mean to. I appreciate the trouble you've gone to with me and if I've said anthing. . .'

He turned to look down at her, standing very still, his eyes piercing even in the gloom.

'You have not offended me. You have fought me since our first meeting and finally you have left me with a rather wet and creased shirt, but I am not offended.'

Jenna looked up, but she dared not look further than the hard chest, the white shirt still showing signs of damp.

'I—I'm sorry. I—I'm sure it will dry soon.'

'You think so?' He suddenly captured her hand and placed it where it had been before, over the steady beat of his heart. 'How long do you think it will take?'

Jenna's face went pale as he held her hand firmly against him. The heat of his body was like a magnet and she knew she would not have been able to move her hand even if he had let her. Her fingers began to move as she watched them almost in a hypnotised way. His skin was warm, the feel of crisp hair beneath the silk tantalising. She felt faint now, but for a very different reason, and she bit down hard on her lip. When she dared to look up she found herself gazing into burning dark eyes, and when she couldn't look away, Alain brought her closer, his arms closing round her as he crushed her against his strength.

'Don't torment me.' She whispered it against the warmth of his neck and he released one hand to spear his fingers in her hair and tilt her face to his.

'It is permissible only for you to torment me?' he asked thickly. 'Do I not have any rights?'

'Alain?' She whispered his name rather desperately and he caught her mouth with his, his lips hardening to demanding pressure when she made no move to resist.

Her head swam as his lips probed hers and she softened even further as his hands began to caress her compulsively. His thumbs explored her ears as his fingertips soothed the back of her neck and as Jenna moulded herself closer his hands moved to her body, tracing her spine and then sliding down to her hips to hold her against him. He had told her that he had wanted her that night at the house, but he needed no words now—his body was evidence enough—and sheets of flame seemed to shoot through her as her arms wound around his neck and she arched against the demanding, hardening muscles.

She had never done this before, never felt like this, but she had no thought at all of moving away. His hands held her to him and their bodies moved together in the most intimate way with no thought of denial.

He suddenly swung her into his arms, his tortured breathing the only sound in the darkened barn, and instead of carrying her down the stairs he turned and lowered her to the soft hay that was spread thickly on the floor behind them. As he gathered her closely back to him there was one second when their eyes met and Jenna saw the open desire in his gaze.

'Are you comforting me?' she asked shakily, her heart threatening to pound out of her chest.

'It's no comfort, *chérie*,' he murmured harshly, 'not yet. Right now it is almost torture.'

Before she could answer he pulled her close again and any thoughts of answering fled as she gave herself up to the excitement. Heated pain seemed to be filling her but it was a pain she clung to desperately, a feeling she had never experienced before. Alain moved until his body was half over her and as his lips explored her mouth his hand moved over her face and neck, searching her skin with increasing ardour until with a low groan he moved right over her, pressing her into the straw as his hands cupped her breasts.

'Say you want me,' he demanded against her mouth. 'Admit that this has been between us since we first saw each other. Tell me you need my hands on you.'

But Jenna was too lost to reality to answer and when he unfastened the buttons on her blouse and found the high, taut peaks of her breasts she tossed her head from side to side in delight as his lips caressed them. When his lips came back to hers, Jenna was soft and pliant, no resistance in her at all, and he rolled on to his back, pulling her over him fiercely and cupped her hot face in strong fingers.

'Come back to Paris with me, *chérie*,' he said heatedly. 'Don't try to deny this feeling between us. I have to go back in the morning and I must have you with me.'

'In the morning?' Her voice and her looks told him exactly how little she wanted to be away from him, and his hands tightened as he rubbed his lips lightly against hers.

'I have to work this weekend. There is a delegation

coming and I must be there. That is why I came today instead. I did not have time to come, but I wanted to see you very badly. Come back with me. I don't want to go without you.'

'I—I have to go back to England.' Jenna had no idea what she wanted him to say to that, but his words sent cold shivers through her.

'Not until you have stayed in Paris with me. I want you and I have no patience to wait.'

'I—I can't leave your mother alone.' She realised she wasn't even thinking about the words that came from her mouth. Inside her thoughts were running around frantically, like the mouse her had called her so tauntingly. He expected her to stay with him in Paris? Sleep with him? It would then be all right to go back to England and Glyn?

Jenna moved and he let her go at once, coming lithely to his feet and helping her up.

'My mother can come with us until I find her a suitable companion.'

'You mean it's all right to sleep with you under your own roof with your mother there although it's not quite the done thing here?' Jenna asked in a hurt voice.

'Jenna?' His softened looks hardened, but she evaded his hands and went headlong down the stairs, stopping only momentarily to brush the straw from her trousers and fasten her blouse with shaking fingers. Alain was beside her as she stepped out into the sunlight and his hand closed around her arm.

'Jenna! Wait!' A car came sweeping into the yard before he had time to say more and they both turned to look, Alain with impatience written across his face and Jenna shaken and miserable.

It was a Land Rover, and when Jenna saw Claudine Rabier at the wheel, her humiliation was complete.

'Alain! *Chéri*! You never said you were coming today.'

She sprang out and raced across with her boundless energy to fling her arms around Alain and hug him close.

'I'm only here for the one night.' He made no move to escape the deadly embrace and laughed down into the girl's upturned face. 'Tomorrow morning I must be back in Paris.' He had fought off his anger, but Jenna could still see it at the back of his eyes.

Claudine suddenly seemed to notice the flustered looks that Jenna still had, although Alain was as cool as if his heated lovemaking had never happened.

'You are both covered with straw, *chéri*,' Claudine said with a glance at Jenna that was pure malice. She began to flick the offending wisps from Alain's clothes. 'I must straighten you up or Marguerite will be shocked and no doubt get the wrong impression.'

'I doubt it,' Alain murmured caustically. 'You were coming to see my mother?'

'In a way. I was intending to get to know your English guest a little more. Marie has been telling me about her. Can I stay for lunch?'

'You must ask my mother.' Finally Alain detached himself from Claudine's clinging hands and turned to the house, collecting Jenna with a very hard hand on her arm.

'Oh, she'll agree. I've always belonged here,' Claudine murmured sweetly. 'Next week I'll come regularly to get to know Mademoiselle Bryant.'

'Jenna is going back to Paris with me,' Alain stated firmly, and Jenna couldn't stand this any longer.

'I'm going back to Paris early with Alain and Marguerite,' she said quickly. 'I have to fly out to England tomorrow. I need the lift to the airport.'

Alain made no sort of sound but his hand tightened to steel and Jenna felt somewhat vindicated. He thought he could simply invite her to sleep with him and she would obey like a lunatic. It hurt. It all hurt, but at least she had now got back at him, and she didn't have to see his face to know he was furious.

For Jenna it was a terrible meal. If either Alain or his mother noticed they said nothing, but Claudine's conversation was utterly empty. She was much too busy darting glances at Alain and then at Jenna and it was not hard to see that she had detected a certain restraint in the atmosphere.

'Did you enjoy seeing your father's studio?' she suddenly asked and it seemed to Jenna that not only did Alain stiffen alarmingly but Marguerite appeared to ice over. Jenna answered before things got out of hand. This girl was too used to getting her own way, but now she had stepped over an invisible line and she didn't even know it. Her little dart at Jenna had infuriated both Alain and his mother.

'Yes. It's fascinating,' Jenna said quickly. 'Alain explained it all to me.'

'Yes, I could see he was doing that,' Claudine murmured sweetly. 'Of course, I knew your father. He frequently wanted to paint me.'

'He was not at all interested in portraits,' Alain corrected, his tight looks relaxing at this obvious, childish spite. 'He painted only two—the one in here of my mother and the other of Jenna when she was sixteen.'

'I imagined he'd never seen her!' Claudine said sharply.

'You imagined wrongly,' Marguerite interrupted with a cold look that was completely at variance with her normally soft ways. 'Jenna lived with her mother, but she was always Russell's daughter and his delight. The portrait of her is, I think, the best thing he ever did.'

'So it must be valuable?' Claudine surmised, a little quietened at this frosty reply. 'Who does it belong to now?'

'It will be Jenna's,' Marguerite stated firmly.

'Oh, but if it's valuable. . .' Jenna's worried voice was interrupted by Alain's harsh intervention.

'It is certainly valuable and I want it for myself. You may state your price, Jenna. I have a vested interest in that painting.'

Of course he had. He was the one who had got the photograph that had enabled her father to do the portrait. She could see why he would want it.

'I don't feel that it's mine,' Jenna said quietly. 'If it is then I give it to you gladly.'

'I do not want gifts, *ma chère*,' Alain said tauntingly, his dark eyes flaring her over. 'I only ever wish to take what is mine.'

Jenna knew she had deserved that sharp slash. She had behaved as if she was quite prepared to be Alain's, and she could not think of any reply at all. If Marguerite noticed Jenna's crimson cheeks she chose to ignore it, but Claudine missed nothing and when they were alone for a moment she turned on Jenna with flashing dark eyes.

'Alain is mine!' she hissed. 'He has always been mine. We are already lovers and soon we will marry.'

'I'm glad for you,' Jenna snapped, standing and looking down at the angry face. 'Please don't hesitate to miss out my invitation to the wedding!'

She walked out of the room and went to her own room, seething with rage, humiliation and a great sense of desolation. Her world was truly altered. Now it seemed there was nothing at all to cling to. She did not need to dig deep to know that she would not be satisfied with her old way of life, with her quiet existence and with Glyn. Being here had awakened something in her. Alain had awakened something too and it could not be dismissed.

She was sitting miserably brooding when Marguerite tapped on her door and came in as Jenna invited her.

'I do not know how much Claudine upset you,' she said quietly, 'but I want you to know she has gone.

Sometimes that girl can be so very childish and quite infuriating. She has been spoiled since birth.'

'Alain seems to like her,' Jenna said gloomily, and got herself a very speculative look from Alain's mother.

'I cannot say he is overjoyed right now,' she murmured. 'When he found you had walked out he said rather pointedly that he would walk Claudine to her car. He is seeing her off the premises at this minute.'

'Did he send you to find me?' Jenna asked, trying not to sound hopeful. It was as well that she had not been because Marguerite looked most sceptical.

'If he had wanted to find you he would have come himself,' she said with a wry look. 'Alain does not stand much on ceremony. He is, as I said, not exactly overjoyed at this moment.'

Neither was Marguerite later. Alain acquainted her with the necessity to leave in the morning and would not countenance any thought of her staying here alone.

'Jenna is going home. She insists on it,' he said flatly. 'This would leave you here all by yourself and I cannot allow that. Pack your things, *Maman*. I imagine that Jenna has already eagerly packed hers.'

Jenna tackled him about that later as Marguerite went up to pack.

'Thank you very much!' she said heatedly. 'Now Marguerite will think that I came running to you to beg to go home. It makes me feel like a sneak.'

'More schoolgirl expressions?' He glowered at her. 'Maybe you have not advanced much from that portrait after all. You wish me to acquaint my mother with the facts? Shall I tell her that you did not come running to me, that instead you melted in my arms after looking at me since I came today with large, yearning eyes? Shall I tell her that your inclination to run came only when I was honest about my feelings?'

'By all means, tell her!' Jenna snapped. He could not embarrass her now, not after Claudine had spoken to her. 'Marguerite already knows her son is a villain, as you told me before. In any case, she would only laugh and not believe a word of it. She surely knows that you are already Claudine's lover. I imagine all the district knows!' She stormed off and didn't wait for any reply, but Alain caught her quickly.

'Idiot!' He looked down at her angry face and burst into laughter. 'You are jealous? Why, *petite*, I never would have thought it.'

'Which is a good thing as it's not even true enough to be laughable,' Jenna bit out. 'Just let it creep through your ten inches of ego-plated hide that I'm not interested in either this place or you.'

'You sound like a woman at last,' he said softly. 'Your body did not lie, Jenna.'

'Maybe it was practising,' Jenna said shortly, and this time when she walked off he let her go.

Dinnertime was a very gloomy affair. Alain was in a black mood and Marguerite was trying hard to pretend she wanted to go back to Paris. Jenna was even tempted to do as she had done before and offer to stay, but this time she held her generosity in check. She had to get away from Alain, to get back to England and some sort of normality.

'What about your inheritance?' Alain said unexpectedly into the heavy silence.

'I've done everything you asked,' Jenna said quietly. 'I've faced the past and I've seen the house and the studio. I have to get back to both my job and my life. Please let solicitors deal with everything, and also, please believe me when I say that I want nothing but a few mementos of my father. This is Marguerite's home and I wouldn't have it any other way. I want you to have the portrait too, as you set so much store by it. I know it's good, but I don't particularly want to be reminded about how life felt at sixteen. In any case, I owe it to you. You took away all the bitterness.'

'Did I?' Alain asked darkly. 'I can still hear it in your voice.' Jenna stiffened, but Marguerite intervened.

'Please, Alain! I cannot face a quarrel and I can see nothing to quarrel about. Jenna has been so sweet to me this week. Surely it is not asking too much to allow her to get on with her own life in her own way?'

'If she knows what she wants,' Alain muttered angrily.

'I do.' When he looked up at her, Jenna met his eyes fearlessly. She also knew what she *didn't* want, couldn't face. She could not face loving Alain and then being left with a smile and a careless shrug. She had been left before when she was eight years old, but if she allowed herself to stay with Alain, to love him, she would not have a whole childhood to recover from it. Self-preservation told her that a whole lifetime might not be enough.

She went upstairs to pack as soon as she could. This time she packed carefully and methodically. She was going to the airport and not to Alain's house. She was going home to England to take up the threads of her life and forget Alain and her time in France. She stopped for a minute and looked out at the fields. She seemed to have known Alain all her life.

Deep inside she seemed to have been waiting like some long-ago damsel in distress, waiting for her knight to rescue her. He had rescued her in his own way, he had swept away the bitterness and the hurt, but he had added a hurt of his own too. He had swept her shell aside and probed every bit of hunger inside her. She turned back to her task impatiently. Who was she to judge Alain? She had been more than willing. She was unsophisticated and shy and she had turned to him eagerly, warmed by his passion, his odd bursts of kindness, his quirks of humour.

It would have to be another lesson learned the hard way, but she could not easily push the thought of him away and she knew she never would. Even before this he had lingered in her mind, seeming to be calling her from

France after that one meeting. How would he seem to be calling her now after she had been entranced in his arms? And what about Glyn? She did not really need to ask herself the question. There would be no Glyn now. Something inside her was singingly awake and Glyn could not even begin to fill the space. It needed Alain, but Alain would not be there.

The ride to Paris next day was not the most comfortable of trips. Jenna sat in the back of the car with Marguerite. She wanted to leave Alain's mother with the very best impression and she knew perfectly well that if she sat with Alain there would be only brooding silence. Alain had been brooding since the night before, and although Marguerite had certainly noticed she had kept quiet.

Even so, there was not much that could be said, other than polite conversation. Both of them were aware of Alain's black anger and Marguerite was feeling the sorrow of leaving her own house. She refused to allow Jenna to feel guilty, though, and from time to time she smiled across and patted Jenna's hand. From time to time, too, Jenna caught Alain's dark eyes watching her through the driving mirror, and she was greatly relieved when they began to skirt Paris.

'Can I be dropped off at the airport?' she was glad to ask as the signs came up. She wanted to be away.

'I must get my mother home first,' Alain informed her bleakly. 'In any case, I have looked up the time of your flight. You have three hours to wait. As I have to come back to the airport to pick up a member of tonight's convention it will be easy to drop you off at the same time.'

There was no arguing with that and Jenna had visions of Alain simply giving her the ride and leaving her to it. Not that she would be unable to manage, but she would have liked to leave in happier circumstances. There was too much anger between them, also too much unhappiness on her part.

She did not want to leave Alain. She was willing to admit that to herself. To leave him angrily was even worse. On the outside he was coolly polite, but underneath he was smouldering with rage. She was surprised how well she knew him and she realised he was perfectly right about one thing: they had recognised each other on sight. She had imagined it was because of her long association with the name Lemarchand, but it was not that. It was an instinctive reaching out to him even when he was a stranger. He was no stranger now and leaving him was hard, more bitter to her than anything had ever been.

The beautiful house looked just the same, white and gleaming in the sunlight, and Jenna looked away quickly, knowing that she wanted to stay here with Alain and not go back to her empty life, her sterile plans for the future. Alain was warmth and power and she needed both, she need *him*.

It was not possible to just sit in the car and wait. Marguerite had to be settled and Alain was determined to see to it. It was also far too early to simply turn round and go back to the city even if Alain had been willing. He was most certainly not willing.

'Coffee, Jules,' he ordered as his servant came to greet them. 'I expect *mademoiselle* would like tea. Bring everything to the small salon as soon as you have it ready. Take my mother's cases to her room later.'

Here in his own house he was aloof, unsmiling, the man Jenna had first met, and it was almost impossible to believe that this man had held her, kissed her passionately, urged her to come here to stay with him. Her face flushed and she turned almost desperately to Marguerite as they sat in the small gold and white salon waiting for their refreshments.

'Do you have any ideas about a companion?' she asked, turning away from Alain's dark gaze.

'Yes. You!' Marguerite laughed. 'I do not suppose, however, that you will be applying for the position so I shall wait for Alain to send a few people here for me to see. It will not be easy. I am not a very social sort of person and I find it difficult to have strangers in my home.'

'You managed with me,' Jenna said with an attempt at lightness, but Marguerite shook her head and smiled softly.

'You were not a stranger, *ma chère*. You are Jenna and I have heard about you always. I even knew how you would look. Also you have Russell's gentle ways. It helped enormously.'

'But now it is over,' Alain bit out. He was standing staring out of the window and his mother looked at him reproachfully.

'Alain! Do not try to make Jenna feel guilty. She had already given up so much of her time to be here. Perhaps she will come back again.'

'Of course I'll come back to the Dordogne to see you,' Jenna promised, knowing as she said it that she could never face Alain again.

Alain turned and looked at her.

'But not back to Paris to see me?' he asked silkily. 'I am to be cut out of this cosy little reunion? I am to be left all alone?'

'Oh, Alain!' Marguerite laughed. 'Do stop getting at Jenna. I know that you two fight from time to time, but let her at least leave in peace. In any case,' she added with a slanting look at him, 'I doubt if you will be alone for long. If Claudine has her way you will be married with some speed.'

'Quite probably.' Alain flung himself into a chair, his lips twisted into the old sardonic smile. 'This time, Claudine was handing out heavy hints that I have kept her waiting too long. I notice she has brought in reinforcements in the person of Villette.'

'He seems quite nice,' Marguerite murmured, her eyes twinkling. They both seemed to have forgotten Jenna and she was glad because she could feel tears welling up inside, almost a feeling of panic. She knew right then that she could not face it if Alain married someone else. Deep down she was almost ready to beg to stay, but her old character came to her aid and she fought for control.

'What do you think, Jenna?' Alain asked cruelly. 'Is Bernard "nice"?'

'I couldn't see much wrong with him,' Jenna answered, forcing herself to look at him. 'Maybe you should take action soon. He was quite charming, the little I saw of him.' She turned away from his scathing eyes. He didn't believe her. He didn't think she could face this with any coolness and she had to convince him. Alain would never know that she was almost ready to break up inside. 'Weddings seem to be in the air,' she said brightly to Marguerite. 'I forget to tell you the other night. When I phoned Glyn, he asked me to marry him. We're getting engaged as soon as I get back to England.'

'How exciting!' Marguerite's rush of words almost drowned out Alain's harsh intake of breath, but he said nothing at all as Marguerite went on, 'Now I know why you could not stay longer. It is not just your lovely school, is it? I'm doubly grateful that you spent the time with me, Jenna, dear, when you were probably pining to get back to your fiancé.'

'I enjoyed being with you,' Jenna assured her, and Marguerite smiled gleefully.

'Then I know you will come back. Bring him with you, *n'est-ce pas*?'

'I will,' Jenna said. She had paid Alain back swiftly and firmly, but she could not turn to face him, and after one look at his tight face, Marguerite glanced from one to the other with suddenly astonished eyes.

* * *

She might just as well have been driven to the airport by taxi, Jenna mourned. Alain would not speak to her. He drove grimly and skilfully and he drove very fast as if he could not wait to get her on the plane to England and out of his sight.

He saw her safely checked in and then left her, his last words calculated to wound.

'So goodbye, Jenna,' he murmured drily, looking down at her. 'I imagine we will be hearing from your solicitor. As French law can be tediously long he may even be your husband before this affair is over.'

'Perhaps so.' Jenna looked down at her toes and then quickly looked at him, wanting to say something to ease this tightness between them.

'Alain. . .'

'Do not pretend, *ma chère*,' he advised coldly. 'I do not pretend, as you see.'

'I wanted to thank you.'

'For what? I have introduced you to your inheritance, given you a glimpse of the man your father was. I considered it to be my duty.'

He was so icy that Jenna's temper flared. He was behaving as if nothing at all had happened between them.

'I assume you considered it to be your duty to kiss me and—and. . .'

'Want you?' he asked softly. 'It was not a duty, *mademoiselle*. It was a pleasure—as far as it went. Will you tell your solicitor about it?'

'It's hardly worth mentioning!' Jenna snapped, her face flushing painfully. He smiled that long, slow, sarcastic smile, but he didn't retaliate. Instead she got a little sardonic bow and he turned and left.

'My visitor has arrived; goodbye, Jenna. It has been interesting. . .'

He just left the remark hanging in the air and she stared after him, the eyes never leaving him at all. It was the last she would see of him, the last time she would be able to watch the lithe way he walked, the way his smile flashed unexpectedly. She wanted to run after him, but it was not at all possible. He had dismissed her.

She saw his visitor because she was not easy to miss—a tall, elegant brunette who smiled radiantly as she saw Alain and who was greeted like a queen. He kissed her hand with more than necessary gallantry and Jenna turned away as jealousy once again bit deeply into her. He did not confine his activities to Claudine, then? Still, as he had said, he was French. What did she know, after all?

As her flight was called, Jenna stood and began to make her way forwards. It looked as if the plane would be full. There would be nobody to meet her in London because she had not bothered to let Glyn know she was coming back. Foolishly she had imagined it would be like inviting herself into a trap, because the trapped feeling was still there. It was only with Alain that she felt free.

She was suddenly wrenched from the barrier, spun round into tight arms and found herself looking into Alain's blazing eyes.

'Alain! What—what is it?'

'A last-minute gift, *chérie*.' He lifted her almost off her feet, pulling her against him and crushing her lips with his. There was so much force in the kiss that Jenna felt faint, the blood rushing to her head and singing in her ears. It was a sensual onslaught that made her brain whirl, and she was still dazed as he released her and looked down into her dazed eyes.

'Call it a wedding gift,' he advised harshly, 'but it is for you alone, not a thing to share with your future husband. I really do not think he would understand.'

He walked off, tall and dark, leaving her standing there with every eye on her. There were amused smiles, but they did not know at all why Alain had done that. Neither did Jenna, but she suspected it was merely anger and frustration. Perhaps she was the only one who had got away? No doubt he had wanted a lot of women.

She walked through the barrier and never looked round. One thing she knew for sure: Alain would be married long before she was. There would be no engagement for her, but she felt that Claudine would cling hard enough and long enough to win. Alain would go on his own powerful way and not change his life one little bit. If Claudine had been just slightly nicer, Jenna would have felt sorry for her.

CHAPTER TEN

JENNA managed for almost a month. The house now stifled her. Where once she had felt secure she now felt alone. Everything she had thought had been a lie and she looked carefully at the things she now possessed with new eyes. There had been no poverty at all, no necessity to move except the necessity of a woman who had been driven by some perverse whim to deny her former husband the right to see his daughter.

For the first time, Jenna searched the house for some sign of her father. She wanted a photograph, a letter, a book that had been his. There was nothing. She even climbed to the old attic that she had never even seen before; perhaps here there would be some painting he had done long ago. If there ever had been there was certainly nothing there now. Imogen Bryant had wiped him out of her life as if he had never existed, and Jenna felt anger at that. It even drove her to going to see Ned Clarke.

'What happened to the paintings my father did before the divorce?' she asked coldly as he invited her to sit. This time he looked at her closely and he could see at once that she was different. There was no chance at all that he would get the upper hand. She was a client and, by the look of her, a very disgruntled client.

'He left them when he left the house. They were part of the contents. Your father agreed to your mother having everything.'

'How do you happen to know all this?' Jenna asked suspiciously. 'It was only in the last years that you knew us.'

'When your mother came to live here and asked me to

advise her,' he said uneasily, 'I naturally wanted to know some background. All previous notes were passed on to me. By then your mother felt fairly safe. Russell Bryant had not been in touch for some time and she seemed to think he had given up.'

'Given up trying to find his daughter, you mean?' Jenna asked angrily. She never for a moment doubted Alain's word.

'I was not involved with that.' The way he flushed told Jenna clearly that though he might not have been involved he certainly knew about it.

'Perhaps not,' she said shortly. 'However, that's not why I'm here. If any of my father's paintings were left behind I want to know where they are now.'

'Sold,' he said distinctly, a rather smug expression crossing his face.

'*Sold*?' Jenna just stared at him, and he nodded with evident satisfaction.

'Your father became well known, as I told you. In later years, his paintings were fetching a great deal of money. I made enquiries for your mother. In France they were much sought-after. She instructed me to get someone to act for her. Shortly after you came to live in this town she began to sell them very discreetly. They were put on to the French market one at a time with intervals between the sales. That way they raised rather a lot of money. That is how she was able to leave such a large amount of cash to you, my dear.'

'So she got rid of every last one?' Jenna felt rage rising. This smug man who had nothing at all to do with her life had helped to wipe out her father's existence for her. 'Where did they go? Is there some record?'

'I imagine so, if I were to dig around in my files.' He glanced across at her with faint amusement. 'However, if you imagine you can now buy them back I would advise you to forget all about it. I told you they sold for a lot of money. Now they are worth even more, especially as he is dead. Even if you sold the house you live in, there is no way in which you could buy back the paintings, even if the owners would sell. These things only rise in value. You should forget all about it.'

'I'll decide about that, Mr Clarke,' Jenna said grimly, standing and looking down at him until he got hastily to his feet. 'In the meantime, please *do* "dig about in your files" and find out who bought them. Send me the details when you send your account.'

'The accounts go out every six months,' he reminded her with a frown.

'I shall need mine sooner,' Jenna said with a wintry smile. 'I intend to change to another firm of solicitors, so naturally I'll want to settle with you. I shall expect all papers and documents to come with the account.'

She nodded coolly and walked out fuming. That someone who had nothing at all to do with her life should have had a hand in removing her father's last trace in her life infuriated her. She knew she would never be able to buy back all the paintings, but perhaps some owner would be willing to sell.

To buy back a few of her father's paintings she would be glad to sell the house and move into a rented flat. It meant a lot to her now because she would never take anything away from Marguerite and Alain. They still had more right than she did to own anything her father had left, but she desperately wanted something, something to be able to look at, something to let her know that he really had existed and that he had needed her after all. Her memories of him were very faint and she needed something concrete to build on. She needed it more than ever now that Alain was gone. In any case, she knew deep down that Alain would want this.

She had already told Glyn that she would never be anything but a friend to him and he had taken it better than she had thought he would. He was, after all, not a passionate man, and the new Jenna who returned from

France had rather alarmed him. There was a blaze in her eyes that had not been there before and he could see at once that she would not be at all manageable. They had parted in a friendly enough way, promising to see each other from time to time, but Jenna very much doubted if it would ever happen. She imagined he looked almost relieved and she felt the same. They were not, as she had once thought, well suited. They had nothing in common at all. Glyn was steady and rather stuffy. She was wildly alive and singing inside, restlessly wanting something she could never have.

School was not the same either, because Jenna found it hard to keep her mind from winging back to France and Alain. Sometimes she came back to the present with a bang to find that one of the girls had asked a question and had received no answer at all because Jenna's gaze was fixed on the sky outside the window, her mind travelling the road to Paris and Alain.

Finally she came to a decision and went to see Mrs Constantine. She would have to leave. She found herself pouring out her unhappiness to that odd but kind lady and when she had finished the headmistress sat back and looked at her sympathetically.

'Go back to France, Jenna,' she advised. 'You can resign in the complete knowledge that should you ever want to come back there will be a position here for you at any time.'

'I'm probably mad,' Jenna confessed with a little laugh.

'They all think that I am,' Mrs Constantine assured her wryly. 'Follow your heart, Jenna, and see where it leads you.'

She knew where it would lead her and she also knew it would bring grief. Alain had been right, though, when he said she would finally come back and search. She had left so much undone. She had never even asked if there was a photograph of her father, and she supposed they had been so careful not to upset her that they had never offered one. She must go back to the Dordogne, back to Marguerite.

Inside she knew she would also be searching for Alain, but she thrust that thought away because there would be nothing there that belonged to her. A month was a long time. He would have put her from his mind. The law would be taking its stately course and perhaps one day she would have to sign documents, but as yet there had been no word from France—even Marguerite had not written—and Jenna felt very much alone.

The farm looked just the same. Jenna pulled up in the small courtyard and sat for a moment looking at it. There were more flowers now and the sunlight was stronger. The feeling was back that at any moment Alain would come, but she knew it was merely dreaming. She had brought her car this time, crossed by ferry and faced the terrors of the Paris ring-road, but she needed her own things with her and this was the only way to do it.

There was nobody at all here. As Jenna stepped out of the car there was only silence and she frowned at her own stupidity. Of course Marguerite would not be here unless she had already found a companion; Alain would not have allowed it. It would have been sensible to have got in touch, but she had been desperate to get back and every mile of the road from Paris had been singingly bittersweet. Now there was nothing, no way of even getting inside the place.

A sound had her spinning round and she found herself looking into the astonished eyes of Marie as the girl slid from her bicycle and walked forwards to confront her.

'There is nobody here, *mademoiselle*,' she said shortly.

'I'm aware of that,' Jenna said. It was strange, but she was not now the old Jenna, shy and anxious. 'However, you're here and I know you have a key.'

'But it is my key, *mademoiselle*,' the girl said defiantly. 'I could not lend it to you.'

'You're not going to lend it to me, Marie,' Jenna said firmly. 'You're going to give it to me. Furthermore, I do not need you to clean while I'm here.' She had made her mind up with little thought. She was here, where she wanted to be. If anyone found out and if Alain was angry she would fight it out later, but for now she had come a long way, she was tired, disappointed, and nobody was going to stop her from staying here.

'I cannot give it to you,' Marie said angrily. 'I have to clean too. *Madame* will be very annoyed.'

'I doubt it,' Jenna said briskly. 'You seem to know a lot about other people's affairs so you probably know that this house is partly mine. I have every right to be here and, as to *madame*, she's my friend. Give me the key.'

It was a question of who would lose her nerve, and Marie could see that Jenna was not about to lose hers. She felt in her pocket and handed the key over with very bad grace.

'Thank you.' Jenna took it firmly and turned away. 'When I leave I'll let you know. I'll take the key to the château and hand it to Mademoiselle Rabier. I'm sure you'll be seeing her.'

Jenna locked her car and walked into the house, closing the door behind her. She had a little smile on her face because she had won that round easily and it gave her a great deal of satisfaction. Claudine and Marie would have a lot to talk about. She looked round with pleasure. It was like coming home and the first thing she did was to walk to the pictures that hung on the wall and look at them all over again. This time she felt they were smiling at her.

'I've come back,' she said softly. 'I understand and I've come back.'

She brushed the tears from her eyes and took stock of

her position. She had brought everything she would need, including a little food as Marguerite was not expecting her. She knew there would be tea, coffee and most other things she would need for tonight. She had collected fresh bread on the way through the little villages and had also bought fruit and vegetables. She might not be able to manage one of Marguerite's culinary delights, but at least she could cook herself a meal. She was a fair cook herself and enjoyed it.

By the time she had got her cases up to the guest room, made the bed up and sorted out her food supplies it was beginning to get dark and, although she had a burning desire to go up to the studio, caution prevailed. Alain had been uneasy about his mother being here alone. He was not in any way foolish and she bowed to his orders as ever. She locked her car, locked the doors of the house and settled down to be by herself. In the morning she would ring Marguerite. The telephone number would be somewhere in the house and in the morning Alain would be at his office and not likely to answer the phone.

The long drive had tired her out and Jenna made her supper and went to bed quite early. It was wonderful to be back in this little room, to know that her father had walked past this door and even been in here. She snuggled down and began to drift to sleep, memories of Alain holding her here as she wept on that first day, memories of him bringing her up to bed after he had kissed her in the kitchen, fluttering like moths in the light, easing her into sleep. In her dreaminess she seemed to be surrounded by love.

Sleep was disturbed by a violent hammering on the door and Jenna shot up in bed, frightened out of her wits. For a minute she didn't know where she was and, as she realised she was at the farm, fear stayed firmly with her. She was alone in this isolated house and not a soul knew she was here except that wretched Marie. Could it be Claudine, incensed that she had come back?

No. It was not likely. If Claudine was incensed then she would have rung earlier and said so.

It had to be someone who had come while she was asleep. It was completely dark and she dared not even put the light on to look at her watch. The violent hammering continued and Jenna crept out of bed to look down into the dark courtyard. She couldn't see anything. It was even too dark for her to be able to see her own car. She would have given anything for a glimpse of the moon that had been shining when she was here before, but it was not there, and as the knocking gathered strength she realised she would have to go down. Whoever it was might just break in and, if they did, she wanted to be on her feet to face them. In any case, she was too scared to go back to sleep even if she had been able to.

Jenna crept down the stairs, pulling her dressing-gown closely round her, stumbling across the room to the door. At a pause in the hammering she gathered her courage and demanded firmly, 'Who is it? What do you want?'

'I want the door open! I probably want to shake the life from you!'

'Alain?' At the sound of his enraged voice Jenna's legs almost gave way beneath her. There was a feeling of relief—that was true—that it was Alain and not some midnight prowler, but also there was a wonderful floating feeling of joy just to hear his voice, no matter how angry he sounded.

'Of course it is me!' he roared. 'Who else would be likely to drive from Paris in the middle of the night and go halfway to demolishing a door? Open up, Jenna, before I break it down completely.'

She rushed to obey, fumbling about hopelessly until her dazed mind ordered her to put the light on. When she finally managed it he just stood there in the darkness and glared at her. He was white with rage and she stepped back rather fearfully as he came inside and slammed the door, locking it securely.

'Why—why are you here?' He spun round from his task at her small query to stare down at her with dark, furious eyes.

'Do not begin to ask me idiotic questions,' he warned. 'I am beside myself with annoyance and not at all in the mood to pander to stupidity.'

'But how did you know I was here?' Jenna drew back and looked at him anxiously. She knew he had not wanted any woman to be here alone, but his rage was more than that surely.

'Claudine,' he said tersely, flinging his coat off and striding through into the kitchen. 'Hysterical messages waiting for me when I got home.'

'I'm sorry if it embarrassed you. . .'

'Embarrassment does not come into it,' he rasped, switching on the kettle and turning to glare at her. '"Enraged" is the word you are looking for, *mademoiselle*. *Mon Dieu*!' he muttered. 'I am starving and thirsty. I have not eaten for hours.'

It was only then that Jenna looked at her watch.

'It's gone three in the morning!' she gasped, and his face told her he was well aware of it.

'I arrived home at midnight after a long and tiresome conference in Lyons,' he grated. 'I was met by my mother in a panic, blurting out your name. By the time I had some sense out of her it was too late to consider having even a coffee. Claudine had phoned indignantly to say that you had taken Marie's key, ordered the poor little thing away and taken possession of the farmhouse.'

'I didn't have any other way of getting in,' Jenna began firmly, but her face fell as she thought of Marguerite. 'Is your mother angry with me?'

'She is not. She is merely anxious. On the other hand,' he added caustically, 'almost every other person involved is furious. That should please you.'

'I wanted to come back,' Jenna confessed. He turned

and looked at her and she hung her head. 'Perhaps I should have got in touch first?'

'It is what a normal person would have done,' he agreed. 'However, "normal" is not exactly a word that fits you, so we will let that one go.'

'I—I'll cook you a meal,' Jenna offered quickly, pleased to see that some of his rage had subsided.

'I am capable of cooking for myself,' he assured her stiffly, and she knew she would have to do a little begging to keep him from another burst of anger.

'You must be tired. I can cook perfectly well. Not like your mother, but by other standards I'm quite good.'

'Are you?' He looked at her derisively and left her to it, drinking the coffee he had made and sitting at the table.

Now she felt nervous. Wherever she went his eyes followed her and she wished he would speak even if it was only a harsh word.

'Something very light,' he ordered. 'An omelette will do fine.' He continued his relentless watching and when the omelette was prepared and she was almost ready to scream he asked, 'So why are you alone? Where is this fiancé of yours?'

'I haven't got a fiancé.' She dished up the meal and carefully avoided his eyes.

'You changed your mind?'

'It was Glyn's idea, not mine, and I think he's glad to see the back of me actually. When things begin moving here you'll have to deal with a new solicitor.'

'Ah! You have cut yourself off from contact with him?'

'Not at all. We're still good friends. It's his partner I can't stand.' Jenna poured herself some coffee and sat opposite, deciding to face things through and not run as she had intended. 'I—I found things out. Anyway,' she added hurriedly, 'it's my business. I can manage my own affairs.'

'Badly. Next time you decide to take some action,

kindly inform me. I don't particularly like driving to the Dordogne through the night with the car almost on two wheels.'

'There won't be a next time,' Jenna pointed out quietly, looking down at her hands, which were clenched around the cup.

'Then why did you come at all?' There was still the hard edge of annoyance in his voice and Jenna gulped back tears. This was not what she had intended. She had never thought she would see Alain. Honesty made her admit she had hoped, but it had been merely dreaming, nothing like this harsh reality.

'Things were different. I—I was alone.'

He was silent and when she looked up he had pushed his supper aside. His dark eyes were burning into her.

'You were alone when I found you.'

'It—it wasn't the same. I built my life on a lie. I know that now. You were right after all. I wanted to search, to come back and find some trace of my father.'

'And only that?' He sounded weary and she was reminded that he must be very tired.

'You should go to bed,' she managed chokily. 'I'll make a bed up for you.'

'I do not feel much like sleep,' he said harshly. He stood and made for the other room. 'Go back to bed, Jenna. It's almost morning. Tomorrow we'll decide what to do with you.'

'You don't have to do anything with me!' Jenna burst out tearfully. 'I can look after myself. I know I shouldn't have come here alone, but there's no need to act as if I'm a personal burden. I just wanted to see the house again, to look at my father's things. I'll go back tomorrow. I never intended anyone to know that I was here except Marguerite.'

'I can understand that,' he rasped. 'I fully realised I was being firmly pushed out of your life when you went back to England.'

'I didn't want to push you out of my life,' Jenna whispered. 'You made it impossible to be just friends. Claudine resents me and when you're married. . .' She was too full of misery to finish and she brushed past him to go to the stairs, not able to face this at all.

His arm shot out and he spun her round, glaring at her.

'I am not marrying Claudine!' he snapped. 'I do not want her; I have never wanted her. She is like a spoiled child.'

'She said —'

'You take her word above mine?'

Jenna looked up at him with tears sparkling on her lashes and then hung her head.

'It doesn't rally matter. I have no real right to be here. You made me feel I had, but I haven't. This is Marguerite's home and yours too. All the memories are yours.'

'Memories can be shared, if that is what you want,' Alain said softly. He lifted her face, cupping it in warm hands. 'For myself, I do not want memories. I want reality.' When she just looked at him his face softened magically. 'I have other memories too, *petite*,' he murmured. 'I remember a pretty girl on a bicycle, a silver bird with sad eyes, a young girl who entranced me. Russell was not the only one to gaze at the portrait. I gazed too. I gazed until I asked myself if I was quite mad. I have known you always, it seems, and when we at last met I felt the air between us stir as if you too knew.'

He gave a wry smile and let her go.

'At least I have given you your past even if I cannot give you your future. You came to find your father; you came back. I suppose it is all I could have expected.'

Inside, Jenna was shaking with hope. She could not really let herself understand what he was saying, but she knew she had to speak out, to let him know it was not just the thought of her father that had brought her here.

'I—I didn't come back just for that,' she confessed,

looking up into his proud, handsome face. 'Nothing was the same any more. I—I felt lost.'

'Torn between two lives,' he suggested, but she shook her head wildly, wanting to confess how she felt.

'No! I wanted to come here because. . .something was missing. I couldn't settle down to my old life because. . .'

'Find your courage, sweet Jenna,' he said softly, taking her shoulders in strong, warm hands.

'I missed you! I needed you!' She blurted the words out, but they were not enough for him.

'And?' He watched her flushed face with intent eyes and she didn't even try to look away.

'I realised that I'll always need you,' she whispered. 'I'll never need anyone else.' She had put her heart on the line, but it was worth it. For a second he just looked into her eyes and then she was tightly in his arms.

'*Chérie*! If you had not confessed I think I would have beaten it out of you.' He tilted her face and looked down at her sternly. 'You have given me a whole month of misery. I have been waiting each day to hear if you had decided to marry that idiot in England.'

'How did you expect to hear?' He had not told her he loved her, but his every action seemed to be saying it, even the tone of his voice.

'I can still afford private detectives.'

'*What*?' Jenna drew back to look at him with stormy disbelief and he grinned down at her, gathering her close again.

'Darling, they did not follow you about. All they were told to do was let me know if you became engaged.'

'I might have,' Jenna threatened, snuggling close.

'I would have been there immediately to create a scene,' Alain assured her. His hand cupped her face and his lips searched for hers gently. 'You were spoken for already,' he whispered. 'When I saw you again I knew why I had waited so long to marry. You were the girl in my dreams.'

Now there was nothing to keep them apart and soon Jenna was too lost in love to remember where she was. All she knew was that Alain was there, holding her, kissing her, his caresses making her faint, and when he lifted her in his arms she curled against him, her lips trailing soft kisses against his strong neck.

'There's only one bed made up,' she whispered as he carried her up the stairs.

'We will only need one,' Alain said huskily. 'Now that I have you at last you'll never be away from me again.' When he placed her on the bed and sat beside her she was left in no doubt of his love. His eyes worshipped her and his voice was gentle as he said, 'I can hold you all night and never go further. I love you, *chérie*. I sometimes think I was born loving you.'

Jenna said nothing but her fingers began to unfasten his shirt, her hands caressing his skin, and soon he was in no doubt about her feelings.

'I've never done this before,' she confessed shakily, and Alain smiled down at her, his hand stroking her hair.

'I know that, *chérie*. You're not much changed from the girl on the bicycle.'

'I'm more fierce.' Jenna found herself smiling into his eyes. The excitement was there, the burning heat inside her, but also there was peace, belonging. This could be joyous because she was safe, at home. She put her feelings into words. 'I'm safe, free,' she whispered.

'Always,' he said huskily. His eyes moved over her, his senses stirring, and answering tingles ran over Jenna's skin, her nipples hardening as his body became tight and sensuous against hers.

'Alain.' She said his name helplessly and he impelled her towards him, capturing her mouth with his, kissing her hungrily and intimately, and she moved urgently against him as his hands explored her body. His low growl of pleasure told her she was pleasing him, and his voice was unsteady as he murmured against her lips.

This time, Jenna. . . I seem to have waited forever for you. *Viens, ma chérie*.'

She cried out as he possessed her. It was like fire, flames that seemed to streak through her and then settle to glowing warmth. Her arms wound around his neck as she clung tightly, her mouth open against his face until they were moving together feverishly towards brilliant light that exploded around them.

'I love you.' Alain breathed the words thickly against her lips, holding her trembling body safely until she relaxed against him, sweet and lethargic.

'Why have I always felt that I knew you before?' Jenna asked when her heart had slowed down and his hands ran over her with the dominance of ownership.

'All the time I spent looking at that portrait, probably,' he mused, his lips curved in a smile of satisfaction. 'I knew your name as I knew my own. Surely such powerful thoughts fly through the air?'

'Sparks flew through the air when we first met,' Jenna pointed out. She was surprised to find that she was not at all self-conscious with him and she moved to nestle comfortably against him when he rolled away from her and propped himself up on the pillows. 'You were angry the moment you saw me.'

'And there you are wrong,' Alain assured her in an amused voice. 'I was stunned to find that you still looked the same and I was very alarmed.'

'Alarmed?' She looked up at him in astonishment and he bent his head to drop a kiss on the tip of her nose.

'Very alarmed,' he confessed. 'My beautiful silver-haired Jenna had grown into a woman, a desirable woman who already had a sort of mystical hold on me.' He suddenly laughed ruefully. 'I was not pleased to meet your lawyer friend. To my great annoyance I found myself jealous. I had carried you around inside my mind for years and here was total stranger kissing you.'

'He wasn't a stranger to me,' Jenna protested. It was

delicious to be close to Alain, to belong to him, to know that all the time she had been alone he had been thinking about her.

'That was the trouble,' he said fiercely. 'I had to get you away from him and have you close to me. That was why I insisted that you come to France. There was also the chance that I would recover from the madness.'

'So you set about curing yourself at my expense?' Jenna asked mischievously, and he lifted her up until she was once again wrapped in his arms.

'It was a vague plan, but it backfired. You fitted into my heart as if a space had always been there waiting.' He curved his hand around her neck and tilted her face to his. 'And you were fighting me from the moment we met again.'

'I was scared. You seemed to be drawing me like a magnet, and there was Claudine, anyway.'

'You were jealous, my darling?'

'It wasn't immediately obvious to me,' Jenna said demurely, and he grinned down at her before looking seriously into her eyes.

'There was not Claudine,' he assured her softly. 'There was never Claudine.'

'There must have been other women,' Jenna began mournfully, but his lips silenced her at once and he kissed her possessively until she began to tremble all over again.

'There will never be other women now,' he promised softly. 'I have my angel.'

For a while they lay in each other's arms, the sweet lethargy claiming them, but as Alain's arms tightened around her and his lips became insistent, Jenna drew back and looked up into his dark eyes.

'You said there was a man,' she reminded him quietly. 'You said that my father knew there was somebody else in my mother's life. Ned Clarke said it too, but I don't remember anybody at all.'

'Your mother was very discreet,' Alain said, his lips caressing her cheeks. 'There was little chance that you would know. When the men I engaged were finding you they turned up information about that too. The man was married and he stayed with his wife.'

'So it left Mother alone,' Jenna mused.

'And bitter,' Alain pointed out. 'I would think that she turned the bitterness against Russell although he was completely innocent. She took a perverse delight in denying his existence, in turning you against him. That way, of course, you would not protest when she moved. In any case, you were a child at first with no say in the matter and later, *chérie*, you were programmed to run.'

'I was, I suppose,' Jenna conceded, and Alain drew her tightly to him.

'You will never run again,' he said fiercely. 'I have you and I will keep you. You are home and safe, right in my arms where you belong.'

Jenna smiled up at him and his face tightened with desire, his eyes burning into hers until she closed her eyes and moved willingly against him.

'I want you again,' he breathed. 'It will be a long time before I can look at you and not want you. It might be forever.'

'I can wait,' Jenna sighed as he gathered her close.

After all, she had waited a long time to belong, but she had never realised she could belong so completely. Alain's lips closed over hers and she felt passion rising to match his own. Tomorrow, she thought dreamily, they would tell Marguerite. They would go back to Paris to the beautiful house, but she would never stop being grateful for the farm in the woods, because here she had found her father and here she had found Alain.

'I'm happy,' she whispered against Alain's face. 'I must have been waiting too. I did have a legacy after all. I think it was you.'

'My angel,' Alain said huskily, stroking back her fair hair, 'of course it was me. It was decided a long time ago and the waiting is over.'

Welcome to Europe

PARIS – 'City of Light'

Capital of France, vitally important to its political, cultural, commercial and intellectual life, yet compact enough to enable you to sample the contrasts of its atmospheric *arrondissements*, Paris is a city where style and vitality are evident on every street corner. The distinctive architecture forms a stunning backdrop to your visit in what must surely be one of Europe's most romantic cities.

THE ROMANTIC PAST

As with so many of the cities of Europe, it was ancient **Rome** that really put Paris on the map. In the time of Julius Caesar the **Ile de la Cité**, one of the two islands on the Seine that form the heart of today's Paris, was inhabited by a tribe of Gauls called the Parisii who called their island Lutetia, and who worshipped the river as the goddess Sequana. It became a Roman colony for the next 300 years, and the Roman street plan determined the future pattern of the city.

As the seat of French monarchy right from 888 AD, when **Euds, Comte de Paris**, became king, Paris has always been at the centre of France's political and social tensions, culminating in the **Revolution** of 1789, when on 14th July the Bastille was stormed and destroyed, and the people took to the streets. The class struggles that ensued were not really resolved by the violence, and the republic was ended when **Napoléon Bonaparte** became emperor in 1804. But there was more trouble to come; after a period of Restoration and two more kings, the nephew of Bonaparte crowned himself **Napoléon III** in 1848 and changed the face of Paris: he and his prefect **Baron Haussmann** virtually took the city apart and rebuilt it in the form of the wide avenues we see today. It was only after the **Siege of Paris** in 1870 that France became a republic again.

Paris's colourful history has of course engendered many romantic tales and legends, including that of the secret marriage of the Breton scholar **Pierre Abélard** and **Héloïse**, the beautiful and intelligent niece of Canon Fulbert, in the early 12th century. Abélard was Héloïse's tutor and they fell in love and married secretly when Héloïse became pregnant; but when the canon found out he had Abélard castrated, and the faithful Héloïse ended her life in a nunnery. The pair met occasionally, and were buried together when they died.

On the other hand there is the 14th-century tale of **Jeanne**, sister of Marguerite of Burgundy who was the wife of Louis X. Jeanne was married to one of the king's brothers, but she was betrayed by her lover and banished for the scandal to the **Tour de Nesle**, now the site of the Palais de l'Institut, facing the Louvre. Jeanne would sit in her tower and look down, watching the people passing by; if she saw a man she liked the look of she would summon him to her room for one night—but, anxious to avoid a repetition of the previous scandal, in the morning she would have the unfortunate lover sewn into a sack and thrown into the Seine!

If, however, your romantic tastes lie in the less gruesome, you may prefer the well-known and tragic 19th-century tale of **La Dame aux Camélias**, used as the storyline for Verdi's opera ***La Traviata***. It is the story of Marguerite Gauthier, a courtesan with many important and noble lovers, who fell deeply in love with the young Armand, and he with her. What she didn't tell Armand was that she was dying of TB, and she was known as the Lady of the Camellias because they were the one flower she could bear to have near her that didn't make her cough. But Armand, in the way of the aristocracy, had a marriage of convenience arranged for him, and when Armand's father went to see Marguerite and explain that her liaison with his son might ruin his life, because she loved him she agreed to sacrifice herself for his sake, and told Armand she no longer cared for him and that he was to leave. He believed her, and it was only later that he found out she was dying and learned of her selflessness; he rushed to see her just in time and they were reunited on her death-bed.

There is no limit to the number of famous artists and writers who have lived and worked in Paris. **Chopin** and his lover **George Sand, Picasso, James Joyce, Arnold Bennett, Hemingway, George Orwell**, the Russian writer **Turgenev**—all these came to Paris in search of inspiration, and it surely can't be any coincidence that they found it. . .

THE ROMANTIC PRESENT—pastimes for lovers. . .

'City of Light'. . . The light of Paris is a very special kind of light, bringing a glow to the most commonplace little square or street. Light is a theme of the city, whether it's the sunshine glinting on the rose window of **Notre Dame**, sparkling on the Seine and flooding the **Avenue des Champs-Elysées**, or the night-time illuminations beckoning lovers to enjoy the city to the full. And if you need any more convincing, go to see the dappled paintings of the **Impressionists** in the beautiful, airy **Musée d'Orsay** and drink in the colour and the sunlight.

Paris is a city that brings the senses to life. It's the kind of city where it would be impossible to list all the romantic things you might like to do and see together—there's simply too much on offer. If you haven't been before, a boat-trip or walk along the **Seine** is the best way to experience the mixture of grandeur and intimacy that is Paris. Explore the **Right Bank**—the very essence of bourgeois respectability, commerce, government and justice; or immerse yourself in the bohemian and intellectual image of the **Left Bank** and imagine yourself as a struggling artist starving in a garret!

But, if getting away from the crowds is more your idea of romance, here are a few suggestions for slightly more off-the-beaten-track pursuits.

The **Marais**, in the centre east of the city, is a quiet area full of tiny streets that retain much of the character of the 17th century; wandering around it, you can peer through imposing gateways into the paved courtyards of the numerous ***hôtels***—large private houses, dating back to the 17th and 18th centuries, when the area had great elegance and prestige. Exploring the Marais, you can let your imagination take flight, and flesh out Paris's noble past in all its glory. Make sure that you don't miss the grand, peaceful **Place des Vosges**, originally the Place Royale, built for Henri IV with a royal pavilion on its south side, but not completed until after his death. Home to many famous people, including the French playwrights **Corneille** and **Molière**, and of course **Victor Hugo**, author of *Les Misérables*, the square's distinctive arcades must have provided ideal cover for many a secret romantic assignation—and no doubt still could!

If you like following in the footsteps of writers, make time to stop for a coffee at the **Café des Deux Magots** or the **Café de Flore**, in Saint-Germain, where Simone de Beauvoir and Jean-Paul Sartre spent many hours philosophising—an old notice in the Flore reminds patrons to replenish their coffee-cups at least once every two hours! Or visit the beautiful hillside cemetery of **Père Lachaise** and get lost in its tree-shaded walks, looking for the graves of **Chopin**, **Colette**, **Bizet**, the actress **Sarah Bernhardt**, **Edith Piaf**, **Oscar Wilde** and even **Héloïse and Abélard**.

But if the buzz of a street market is more your style, try the **Clignancourt** flea market in the north of the city, or take a stroll down **Rue Mouffetard**, south of the Latin Quarter, a downhill cobbled street packed with food stalls. And while you're in the area, if the crowds begin to press, just dodge east across Rue Monge to the **Jardin des Plantes**, Paris's pretty botanic garden, and then stop for a refreshing mint tea in the café of the Paris **mosque**.

In fact, Paris must be one of the easiest cities in which to find refreshment: the abundance of pavement cafés means you can always linger over a ***café crème*** whenever you get tired. French food is among the best in the world, and the best value for money can be had if you eat your main meal at midday, when many cafés offer a **plat du jour** or daily special. If time is short and you need to eat 'on the run' there are plenty of snacks available: try a

croque monsieur (toasted Gruyère and ham sandwich) or ***croque madame*** (the same with a fried egg on top); and ***steack frites*** (steak and chips) is always available—but if you like your steak medium, ask for it '*bien cuit*', as the French prefer their meat rarer than the British!

For a romantic special meal, though, you could try oysters (***huîtres***) or rabbit (***lapin***), or a ***steack tartare***—raw minced beef with a raw egg, onions and capers, which is much nicer than it sounds—accompanied by some of the finest wines in the world.

Do you really need any more convincing that Paris is romantic?

DID YOU KNOW THAT . . .?

* the château of **Versailles** was built because Louis XIV, the Sun King, disliked living in the Louvre and found Paris too cramped and dirty.

* the **Latin Quarter** is so called because it houses the university, the Sorbonne, and Latin was the language spoken by the scholars.

* you can visit Paris's **sewers**, *les égouts*—though that may not exactly be the end to a perfect romantic weekend!

* the French currency is the **franc**.

* French lovers murmur '*Je t'aime*' to the one they love.

LOOK OUT FOR TWO TITLES EVERY MONTH IN OUR SERIES OF EUROPEAN ROMANCES:

A PART OF HEAVEN: Jessica Marchant (Bulgaria)
Falling in love with Nikolai Antonow was easy. But Mallory wasn't the person Nikolai thought she was—what would happen when he found out the truth?

CALYPSO'S ISLAND: Rosalie Ash (Malta)
On the romantic island of Malta, Caroline threw caution to the winds and fell in love. But could she trust Roman when he told her that she wasn't just a holiday diversion?

ROMAN SPRING: Sandra Marton (Italy)
Nicolo Sabatini *claimed* that his interest in Caroline was merely that of an employer. So why did he seem to be taking over her life?

LOVE OR NOTHING: Natalie Fox (Balearics)
Ruth had loved—and lost—once on the beautiful island of Majorca. But, this time, she was determined to win Fernando's heart once and for all. . .